WREN GREYSON

A Summer of Static

A Sci-fi Novella

Contents

For Rowan, Aspen, and Shay

Charlotte, NC

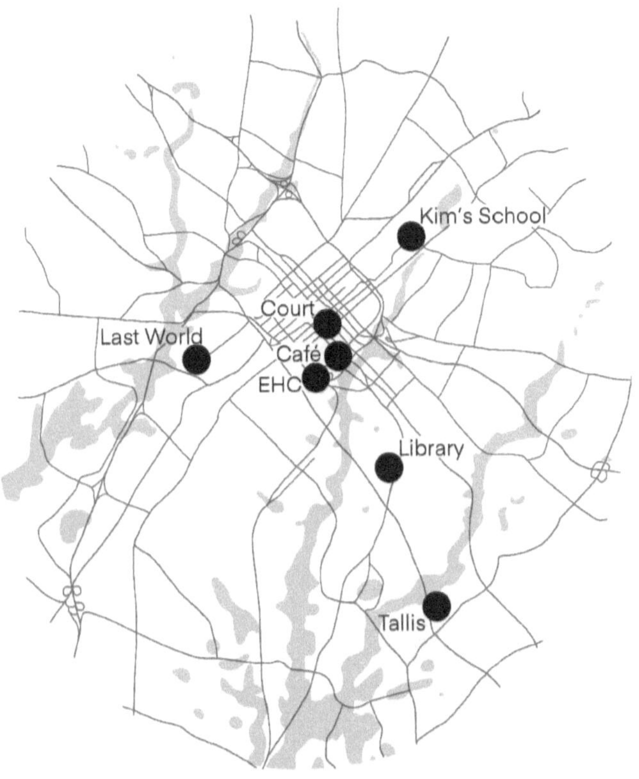

A Summer of Static

Chapter 1

The curtain opens, and Purcell steps out into the light.

They bow once before sitting down. The crowd hesitantly claps like they're not sure they should be, then quiets once they rest their hands on the piano.

Purcell knows they're going to play perfectly. They've been practicing these songs for months.

They take one last deep breath, hold it, count the opening rhythm in their head, and play.

The weight of the keys is familiar under their fingers, and the lurching pedal stays placed firmly under their foot. They smile as they perform, leaning and syncing their body to the music.

Their songs pass quickly. They're barely thinking as the muscle memory guides them through each section. Instead, they take note of how their lucky ring on their middle finger flashes in the lights overhead and how they have ice cream in the fridge at home to celebrate tonight.

This venue is close to their house, so they drove here instead of taking a train like they normally would before a concert. As they perform the last song, they look forward to hopping in their little red car and sleeping in their own bed tonight.

When it's over, Purcell hesitates to lift their hands. There's an odd film over the white keys like they stared up at the lights too long, and it left an afterimage.

They try to blink it away, lift their hands, feel the room inhale, waiting to applaud.

Purcell sits back to stand, but their back hits something where there should be open air. And that afterimage just won't go away.

The applause starts, but it's wrong.

"Hello? You're alright," a man's voice comes from the shadow, which they try to wipe from their eyes again. "Whoa! Be careful! You might scratch your glass!"

Some faraway force is restraining their arm, like they're being pushed underwater.

They wrench their arm out of its grip, hitting their face by accident, and release a startled noise that they can't feel in their throat.

The rumbling applause for their performance hasn't stopped, but they're no longer seated at the piano.

A man's face comes into focus, someone they don't recognize, bearded but young, with clothes covered in oil and grease stains, and a worried expression.

"I'm Tallis. You're alright. Try to slow down. It's okay."

Purcell tries to take a deep breath, but their diaphragm is frozen. They panic at the choking sensation and move to tear at whatever is immobilizing them.

Everything feels *wrong*, far away, abstracted. Purcell is sure it's from shock, but they've never been this disoriented before. They don't drink—don't go out with friends. They're pretty sure they haven't been kidnapped. Nothing explains how they're in this messy garage filled with metal junk and a man they've never met. He's trying to keep their hands from ripping their restraints off.

But then they really look at their hands. They look at their body.

They've been forced into some metal shell, with silver and chrome pieces where their torso should be. There are gaps of nothing on their sides where organs should go, a thinner frame than would fit their skeleton at a bare minimum. Their hands are lifeless and cold material where they should be flesh and blood.

"You're safe. You were in a simulation."

Chapter 2

"Get the fuck off me!" Purcell rips their arms out of the man's loose hold. They start prying at the strap across this weird, shell-of-a-body that they're filling.

The man sits back and watches.

After several embarrassing, futile seconds of animating these limbs that they can't feel, they stop. They sigh, or try to. A hissing exhale like steam sounds, and they glare at their captor.

"Release me."

He winces, almost believably apologetic, and shakes his head. "Are you going to hurt yourself again?"

Purcell scoffs and looks away, but a staticky crackle comes out. They want to say *No*. This body isn't them anyway. They need to escape as soon as possible, get whatever drugs he's given them out of their system, and go home.

They remember what he said—*You were in a simulation.*

They refuse to even entertain the idea. Clearly, *this* is the simulation if they've been stuffed into a robot body like some bad, body-horror movie.

"I'm going to let you out," he prefaces as he reaches forward.

Purcell flinches away. Their shoulder blades dig into the metal chair, and they wince as metal shrieks on metal.

"But you have to promise not to hurt yourself again, okay?"

"What do you mean 'again'?" They sigh in relief after the clip of the restraints hits the stone ground.

They recognize now that the humming background noise they thought was applause is rain against the metal roof.

The man's hand startles them as he goes to touch their face, and they grab his wrist in one of their creepy, skeletal ones.

"Easy," he says, like he's calming a horse. "You left a scratch here. I'll have to fix it later." His fingers trace a path from where their lips were to where an eye should be.

When his hand is this close, it highlights how zeroed in their vision feels. They can't manually unfocus their eyes like they often do when overwhelmed.

"Not that that's a problem, I mean. I'll just have to—I meant that you should be *aware*, you know. That you can scratch it. I can order a lens protector later if you want."

"I need to get out of here—go home." They move to stand and accidentally lurch forward too quickly. "*Oh*, God." They groan as the world moves too fast.

He catches them in something too close to a hug.

Before they can tear away, he lets go first this time. Smart man.

"What was your name again?" they ask. They take note to commit it to memory so they can report him for kidnapping.

They hope they can run out of here without any violence. He seems more delusional than dangerous. Maybe he's a fan of theirs.

"Tallis," he repeats.

Purcell waits for a last name, but he never gives it.

"What about you? I'm assuming P-5370 isn't right?" He gestures to their arm. "How old are you, by the way? That model is pretty old."

His words fade into the droning rain as they examine the arm. It moves when they move, but they've settled on the fact that they're probably drugged.

There's an indented stamp under their forearm—the part that would rest on a table—that reads PRL-5370. It's so close to their actual name; their subconscious must be playing a sick prank on them. They rub the title with the cold, lifeless fingers. They register the movement but still can't feel their skin. Or *metal*, whatever.

"Purcell," they finally answer. "But surely you knew that."

"What?" He tilts his head. Dark curls move with him, and they're jealous of how he probably feels the hair falling to touch his face.

"When you took me? Why did you do it? Where are we?" They start backing away, aware that they need to try to run subtly because his fingers twitch by his side to grab them again.

"I found you. There's a... collection center nearby, and I could tell you were still in good condition."

"What?" They curl their lip in disgust, although they're sure it's mottled somehow. They tense up to run before they get all the information they need.

There's something wrong with this man—*Tallis*, they remind themselves.

"Not that I would have left you if you weren't! I'm just saying that you woke up so easily after—"

"How long have I been here!?"

"Um... A while." He reaches out to stop them after they gasp and stumble backward.

"What did you do to me!?"

"Nothing!" He yells for the first time, although it's out of necessity to be heard over the rain as the two get closer to the open garage door. "You were in a simulation! I don't know for how—probably a long time if you're so disoriented!"

"The hell I was! Put me back in then!"

"I can't!"

Something breaks inside them. They imagine a little circuit board snapping and bouncing off the walls as it falls out of their chest cavity.

They turn on their heel, almost fall over, and have to steady themselves for a precious second they could have used to escape.

"Wait! You're not waterproof yet! You'll—"

"I can't go out in the rain!?" They yank their hand out of his grip again and ignore the thrum of guilt when he winces in pain. "Fuck this! Fuck simulations! Fuck you!"

"No, no! Stop! I—"

Purcell makes it a single step before their vision goes black. They can still hear the rain and Tallis's muttering as he drags them back into the shitty garage.

"God, what have I done to help you?" he says under his breath.

They're not sure how they can hear it.

Then he's across the room as he rifles through metal drawers for something. They can't feel or see anymore. They'd almost believe he hit them over the head with something if they couldn't hear him toweling them off.

Something clicks at the base of their neck, and they panic at the thought of more restraints. Then there's another, softer click of a button behind them, and they're asleep.

Chapter 3

"Okay, attempt two."

Purcell flinches at the sudden torrent of information.

The air has little dust particles spinning in it. Tallis is on a rolling stool beside them, and he's rubbing his palm like it aches. He has thick, dark eyebrows that pinch up in worry and hide behind some of his curly hair. He examines them closely as they wake up.

Though they feel less like they've woken up and more like they've become aware of having already been awake. It's like the world's worst ice bath—suddenly just being on.

"How are you feeling?" Tallis asks as his hands anxiously flicker across them.

They wonder if they should kill him. Obviously, he needs help if he thinks that he's rescued them somehow. It might have been cruel to hurt him if he wasn't holding them here against their will.

"Peachy," they answer. The reminder of food makes them feel worse. They're not hungry, but that's never stopped them from stress eating before.

"Can I leave?" they ask.

"Um… In theory."

They glare.

"I'm… I want you to be safe. You still seem… Tell me about yourself."

They fight not to sigh and look around as they think. It's sunny outside now. Small shafts of sunlight pierce through where metal panels overlap to form the garage, making it look striped. Every flat surface is covered in mechanical parts, tools, all kinds of junk.

"You first."

Tallis takes a deep breath like he's trying not to sigh. "Okay. I'm Tallis. We're… in my garage. I repair robots for a living." He pauses like that's enough, but they stay silent.

He rubs at the calluses on his hands as he looks around with them.

While he looks over their shoulder, he adds, "I graduated the third time two years ago—all mechanics and humanities focused. Um…"

"Humanities?"

His thick eyebrows shoot up. His wide eyes make him look a lot younger. "It's um, history kind of. Sociology, history, and uh… like the way people think and change instead of the events themselves."

"Hm." Purcell nods. Talking feels strange. There's no vibration in their throat or sensation of their own mouth. It feels like music is playing as they think—projecting for them around their temples.

They look down at their body. It's that metal frame from last time. Its joints are visible spheres, protected by candy-shell-looking chrome. Their wrists are strapped to the chair's arms. They can't feel the frayed cord on their skin. *Not* skin.

"You're waterproof now."

They look up to see him pointing out their chrome pieces.

"If one of them breaks, though, water will seep in and lock up the joint."

He stands and motions around their face as they fight not to flinch. "This is silicone. Way more secure. If anything peels off, I'll glue it back, but as long as you stay out of direct sun for too long, then you should be okay."

They blink in disbelief at his strange demonstration, or they want to. Their vision doesn't blink out at all.

Tallis stares down at them, but then takes a step back when they make eye contact.

Their head makes a disconcerting *clunk* against the back of the chair.

"How are you feeling? Willing to talk to me?" As he asks, he undoes the straps on their wrists.

"Fine…" They grumble and grab their wrists after they're freed, even though they didn't hurt. "My name is Purcell. I… I think you're crazy, and I'd like to go home."

They jerk their feet and feel resistance around their ankles.

"Yeah." Tallis puts his hands on his hips as he surveys them. "What's the last thing you remember?"

"You whining like a bitch while dragging me back inside."

"Oh, I meant before—In the simulation." He doesn't show any indication that he's upset by their jab.

Purcell huffs and watches their fingers bend. The chrome beads around their knuckles disappear when their hand is flat and reveal from inside the metal when they bend.

"I was in my real body, looking at my *real* hands. I tried to stand and realized I was tied to this fuckin' chair." They tug at the rope on their ankles while they glare at him.

They could bend down to undo them, but he's close enough to stop them immediately.

"Yeah? Human hands? Like this?" He shows them his own palm—flesh and blood.

"Obviously."

He shrugs as he thinks and scratches the scruff on his face.

Purcell lurches forward to undo the ropes, but slows after feeling their chest clang against their thighs with no resistance.

"Ugh," they groan as they push through the disorientation to tug at the metal clip. They have no idea how to undo it anyway.

Tallis steps forward and gently replaces their hands with his own. He undoes the straps and pulls the cords off completely to put them in a desk behind him.

Purcell jumps up to run, but his sudden acceptance makes them stall. "What's wrong with you? You've put a tracker on me or something?"

He whirls around to answer, but doesn't look upset to see them backing toward the exit. "What? *No.* I wouldn't—I don't want to trap you here. Just... come back if you need help, okay?"

"Sure," Purcell lies. They think to grab their keys and phone, then feel a sharp pang in their chest when they remember those things aren't here. They want their jangly key chain with the little capybara plushie and strawberry charm. It feels strange leaving someplace without their phone, with its worn-out case and its new wallpaper of some wildflowers they recently took.

Does he have their things stashed away somewhere? Is it safe to ask for their stuff, or will he affirm they're not even a human being again?

They turn on their heel and run.

The garage door is open, so they follow the path out to the left of it. It's easy to pick out from the thick underbrush that surrounds them. They feel like a mouse crawling out of a dense, emerald thicket.

The once-gravel path away from the building is all sandy dirt now. The road winds next to a river, and they run until they're certain the only footsteps they hear are their own.

They're facing a bridge and a city on the other side of the river. The bridge rises so high above them that they can't tell if any cars are on it.

Purcell turns to see the garage and gasps at how far in the distance it is already. They can just make out the metal roof sticking out of the grass and coastal plants feeding off the river water. If they hadn't just come from there, they would think it's abandoned.

Maybe it is, and this has all been a nightmare—a hallucination.

They follow the asphalt road that the dirt one merged with. The walk is long, but they're preoccupied with watching their knees bend and their kickstand-like feet propel them forward.

Eventually, they reach the bridge and discover the terribly busy highway that it contains. Most of the cars are going into the city, same as Purcell. The other side of the road only has the occasional 18-wheeler.

Reading the logos printed on the sides of their containers pulls something at the base of their skull, leaving them unbalanced and lost. An eerie familiarity is lapping at them, but they ignore it.

The highway noise drowns out their thoughts, and they miss it once they reach the city, when it disperses into quieter streets. For several minutes, they stand at a corner and watch.

They watch the people in their cars. They watch the occasional pedestrian walk by. The tires rolling on asphalt. Trash moving in the wind. And even a tiny patch of flowers growing along the broken seams of a foundation.

Most of all, they stare at their reflection in the glass. Where their face should be, there's a screen.

It's green with a stupid, mock, pixelated expression. Their flat line for a mouth occasionally twitches in disapproval.

The more they stare at it, the more the green fades into yellow.

Maybe after sleeping tonight, they'll wake up back home.

Sleeping tonight. Purcell curses under their breath.

They spin around to read signs. They need a hotel.

"Fuck." They move to rub their eyes and instead smack their fake face. They have no money. A hostel? Even hostels aren't free.

They glare at their reflection one more time before stomping further into the city, and find a strange pleasure in seeing that their screen is red.

They pass several hotels, but they all look prestigious enough to turn them away for asking for directions, much less for trying to stay.

Purcell grumbles and marches through the thickening crowds. The streets are covered in just as many robots as people. They all give Purcell a wide berth when they can and an apologetic smile before intentionally turning away when they can't.

For some reason, the other robots don't look like Purcell. They have thicker limbs and rounder faces, not the dumb stick limbs and flat screen face that they're sporting. It makes them feel even worse.

Blindingly-white steps grab their attention, and they instinctively wince and try to squint, but nothing changes. They almost walk past the offensive staircase on principle, but then they read the front. Charlotte Mecklenburg Library.

They pivot off the main road, almost walk into oncoming traffic, then head inside. The intense soundproofing blankets them after the door shuts. It's busy here too, and Purcell pushes past the group standing in the way of the door with an upset, stiff-shouldered walk.

They follow a map taped to one of the bookshelves to find the computers. One of the stations has a skewed chair despite looking open. They take it and read the page left open on it.

'WolframAlpha - Math Input
$x(9-x^2)^{1/2}$
Roots: $x=-3$, $x=0$, $x=3$'

They close the tab and click on 'Recent News' instead.

'Jerome Callady, former Aloe star, sentenced to 7 years in prison', 'Canadian nationals charged with smuggling 1.2 billion in illegal whale meat', 'Castillo pardons diver who cut power during Arcadia flood'.

They click on 'WORLD' and skim 'Search relaunched for Cole Falcon, who disappeared in 2082', 'Casualties arrive at hospital after seawall breach in Macau', and 'What to know about Castillo and Palyku with manganese mine'.

They click 'SCIENCE' and read 'The best robots you can't buy in the US', 'Sentience or personhood—referring to our robot allies', and 'Analysts say IRLs showing first signs of sentience'.

Purcell closes them all to stare at the blank, default, blue wallpaper for a moment.

This is a very elaborate dream.

"'Scuse me, hon. Have you seen an old lady walk this way?" A woman taps the wooden barrier around the computer station to get their attention.

Purcell blinks a few times, shocked by the first person to speak to them in hours. "Uh... No, sorry."

"Oh, that's alright." She waves them off and continues down the aisle. She leans hard with every step because of a prosthetic leg. Her long skirt hides exactly how high it goes, but it's at least to the knee—a floral-patterned, metal shell limb.

It's beautiful. It's nothing like Purcell.

Maybe that's what happened to them. Shoved into an entire prosthetic body, piece by piece, replaced until all that's left is their brain.

Purcell frowns and types in 'simulations'. A long list of ads and sponsored products pop up. They scroll past things labeled 'Farmer sim, realistic', 'Cafe sim, cozy', and 'Famous sim, feels just like real life!'

They refine it to 'simulations explained' and scroll until they find a link to a PDF used at Queens University.

> *'Simulations are false realities, similar to virtual realities (VR), with a focus on sensation and realism. They were first designed as a commercial-use alternative to Paid Time Off (PTO) in 2038, but they have since been developed into a wide range of educational aides and experiential learning.'*

Purcell skims some of the subheadings after the abstract. 'Introduction, Background, Applications, Virtual and Reality, Agency Concerns, Dangers and Mental Health Concerns'. They click the 'Dangers' right away.

> *'Despite simulations' many educational benefits, they*

have raised a few mental and ethical concerns since their first global implementation in 2038. Introducing simulations as an alternative to vacation hours created a significant backlash, as we have mentioned, but even at its best, the use of simulation realities can cause a lot of damage to the human mind. Several studies have shown dangerous levels of dependency, post-simulation disorientation, post-simulation depression, and increased risk of anger-related disorders and violence have all been observed.'

Purcell huffs and scrolls faster as they skim the rest of the article. 'Evidence of memory loss as a result of disorientation after long-term immersion', 'recommended treatment is a slow reintroduction to the real world, implementation of mindful habits and hobbies, and group therapy', and 'typical emotional responses as a result of a sudden loss of a simulation include anger, hopelessness, loss of sense of self, and dysphoria'.

They close the tab to look up nearby hostels, but there are none.

They try to rub their eyes again, and the *clink* as their fingers hit the glass makes them groan in frustration.

"You alright, honey? I ain't seen one o' y'alls kind in a while." A slightly-too-loud voice comes from their right again.

Purcell turns and flinches at the old woman peering over the wooden barrier to see what they're doing. She has purple hair, thousands of soft-looking wrinkles, and squinty yet bright eyes.

"Um… Hello?" Purcell says after the woman keeps staring.

"Y'alright?" she asks again.

"Oh. Yes, of course. Thank you." They feel unbearably seen

by this woman. "I think someone is looking for you, actually. With a metal, flowery leg?"

"Ah. That'd be my daughter." She waves off the matter like a pesky fly. "You can't lie very well, 5370."

They flinch back in shock. She walks around the short wall to get close enough to pat their shoulder. They're numb to it, but they appreciate the gesture nonetheless.

"There's a free housing deal nearby. They'd let you in for sure."

"What? How did you know I'm…" They can tell by her amused smile that she isn't going to answer. "Even when I look like this?" They gesture at their whole body and cringe when the woman follows to look them up and down.

"Of course, hon. It's pretty obvious talkin' to you that you've got some'n goin' on up here." She affectionately pats their metal head.

"As opposed to…?" Purcell tries to ask kindly.

"Not all robots have their own minds. Sentience—they call it now. Some o' ems just programmin'."

"Ah. That… makes sense." Purcell nods and turns back to their computer, then feels like an idiot when they read the article where they left off. 'Top-Rated Hostels 2100'.

"Go 'head and type in EHC," the old woman waves them on.

"Okay… This one?"

"Mhm."

They click the link titled 'The Essential Home Cover'.

"There you are!" The daughter whisper-yells once she turns a corner. "I was looking all over for—Oh. Hi."

"Hi," Purcell says flatly back. They hope she doesn't think they lied earlier. "Thank you for…" They wave at the Essential Home page and wait for the woman to leave.

"Ah, it's no trouble. More people should know 'bout that place," she says with a firm nod that clearly says, *I'm not leaving.*

"The EHC? I'm Crystal, by the way." The daughter offers her hand.

"Purcell, nice to meet you."

"Oh, that's pretty. 'S an old name too."

"Yeah?" They wonder why their dream is making them such an outsider. They have friends back home, kind of. Their subconscious shouldn't be too lonely, especially enough to conjure up this whole mess.

"I'd offer to walk with you, but—" The old lady shrugs before they even have time to argue.

"Oh no, no. Please. Don't worry about it. I'm having an easier time walking around anyway after—" They gesture again to their weird, mechanical body.

"Recent upgrade? I've never seen one of your models working so smoothly before. Most of them are... in museums." Crystal clearly intended to say something like *dead* or *out of commission,* but caught herself in time.

"Um... kind of." They flex their fingers to look at the new chrome plating over their rust-prone joints.

"That's nice. Wish we could do that. Closest I've got is this thing, but it's causin' me more problems than it's worth," Crystal complains, and some of her accent slips through like her mom's.

"Yeah? Does it not work right?" Maybe that's why the knee hadn't bent earlier.

"No, no. It'd work fine if I was just a little taller. Damn doctors gave it to me on Condition 3 but won't give me a new one without makin' me pay extra. 'Cause in all their records it fits fine and does what it needs to do," she grumbles, and her mom somberly nods.

"Could you have it shaved down a bit, so it's shorter?" Purcell offers.

"Maybe. But I'm scared to break it. Then they'd be sure to say it was my fault."

The mom leans in to ask them something. "What about where you go to get patched up? Surely, whoever keeps a PL running will know how to break a leg." She laughs at her performer joke, and something deep in Purcell's chest wants to be angry. Or maybe to cry.

They miss being on stage and getting cheered on. They should be bowing to a crowd and being praised for another performance well done, not looking up how to survive with no money in a big city.

They take a shaky breath, which feels like nothing at all, before shrugging and searching for 'Tallis'.

After multiple refined searches and still no promising results, they give up.

"I'm not sure. He's in some rusty, old shed on the other side of the bridge."

"This southeast one?" The mom gestures behind her, and Purcell nods.

"Jeez, that's a long way. You don't have someone closer?" Crystal asks.

They fight not to glare. This feels more like an interrogation than a friendly conversation. "Not yet," they grit out.

The old woman laughs and pats her daughter's shoulder. "You're fine. We're gonna get out o' yer hair now, but you make sure to check out that place, a'right?"

"I will. Thank you."

"Thank *you*, sorry! Good luck!" Crystal waves, and Purcell

can see she's genuinely embarrassed, so they smile and wave back.

Silence seeps in after the two leave. Purcell sits like a stone, building the courage to turn and eventually leave. They memorize the location of the EHC because they don't have their phone. It aches again that they can't just call someone for help.

They restart the computer, push in their chair, and head downstairs.

Chapter 4

Purcell is about ready to pull their nonexistent hair out after reading a sixth article on simulations with zero helpful information. They can't find anything on how to re-enter a simulation that they haven't recently purchased.

All the advice online starts with downloading a sim-life, and they don't know what to search for being human either. Typing in 'I don't belong here' gave them a mental health warning and nothing useful.

They groan loudly again before pushing to stand, accidentally knocking their chair down, then catching themselves with their bad arm. Their left wrist is malfunctioning after they mindlessly picked at the bumpy wires for the hours they spent reading. Even worse, their fingers can feel sensation now on that hand. So they feel the exposed nerve-fire that comes after landing on it.

Purcell curses and ends up on the floor anyway as they curl up around their damaged hand. They feel like seething expletives through their teeth, but the best they get is their apartment lighting up red as their face reflects their mood.

They discovered last night that it becomes a stony gray when they're focused, and a creamy orange when they're surprised.

They stand and right their chair once they can ignore the

feeling of grabbing a hot iron. Maybe they should find someone who can help in the area. Although the idea of going to some kind of mechanic instead of a doctor feels more barbaric than asking a veterinarian to give them a check-up. At least their body *here* is injured and not their real life, where they need their actual hands to work as a pianist.

They mutter vulgar editions of "Why me?" as they stuff their wires back into their wrist themselves and then gag at the visual.

Their apartment lights up a yellow-green, and they close their eyes to calm down, but nothing changes. They sigh and reach up to cover the camera at the top of their faceplate. Then the world comfortably fades to black.

Purcell takes a relaxing minute to do nothing, but it quickly turns into their mind racing about how long they'll be stuck here. Are they in a coma or something? Why can't they wake up? They want to bow after their performance, get takeout during the drive home, and relax on the sofa with wine and a blanket until they eventually doze off and move to their bed around 2 a.m., like they always do. After this nightmare is over, they might even treat themselves to an order-in instead of takeout so they can drive straight home.

Purcell's tense shoulders fall at the thought, and the dull *clank* as their metal hand hits their head ruins their daydream. They open their eyes by moving their hand away from their camera, and scan their very plain apartment provided by EHC.

As soon as they found the business, it was easy to introduce themselves to the front desk staff and get a key to a Condition 3 accommodation. It almost felt like checking into a hotel, minus the payment and required check-out time.

Purcell was happy to read that this place also provides meals in the office four times a day, but they've since realized that they don't get hungry anymore. They have cravings (God, they want Chinese takeout so bad), but they don't feel hungry. Or thirst, or fatigue. Well, physical fatigue anyway. They sure as hell wish they could take a nap, but when they tried, they ended up just lying on a bare mattress and feeling like they were watching paint dry. There's no telling if that's another part of being in a robot body or if they can't relax, but they're getting the feeling that it's a fun, new feature of theirs.

It's noon now—their first full day of living in this apartment—and they don't know what to do.

There are footsteps and conversations in the hall outside every few minutes, and they're tempted to poke their head out their door to demand some stranger to tell them where they're going, how they're doing it, and what they can do to help them get home.

Purcell paces the kitchen, close to their front door, when they spot another cobweb that they missed while cleaning earlier. It's under a cabinet, near the floor.

They bend down to wave it away with their fingers, and cringe when they realize that what they thought was a stain on the cabinet is actually some kind of congealed, mystery goop. They scratch it off the door and accidentally score the wood.

They hesitate to move to the sink. It doesn't work, or at least it didn't last night. They try the knob just for fun, sigh in acceptance as it sputters air at them, and then walk to use the bathroom sink to wash their hand instead.

They asked the staff member last night why they're given all these utilities that they're never going to need, but she had blinked at them, confused. Then she explained that robots often have humans visit or live with them, so it only makes sense that they would want to be hospitable for friends who do need a toilet, shower, fridge, etc.

She'd said it kindly, but how slowly she spoke made Purcell want to walk back into traffic.

They look in the mirror until their screen changes from a desaturated red into a navy blue. They think it means that they're calm.

Before turning off the computer, Purcell decides to search for something they've been meaning to but keep forgetting.

'What is Condition 3?'

The results all agree finally, not the barrage of differing opinions that their previous searches were giving them.

> *'Condition 3 is a needs-based service assigned to all peoples who are underage, unemployed, recently injured/disabled, refugees, and any other status condition that requires their sentient rights be provided at the minimum effort or cost to a firm/region/municipality in order to be fulfilled.'*

Purcell squints at this for a moment before clicking on a much shorter result. It takes them to a student's study guide.

'Condition 3 is the lowest level of aide that people can get from the gov't. (Given to kids, disabled people, robots, homeless). There are some exceptions like if they're accompanied by an adult or if they correctly filed for a higher level of importance.'

With that slightly insulting, though much clearer, definition explained to them, Purcell decides to go for a walk.

Chapter 5

The muscle memory of getting in line after spotting a nice café makes Purcell freeze from embarrassment. They can't back out now. That would be even worse than the fact alone that they've already gotten in this damn line.

They resign themselves to just commit for now, but they see a break in the barrier of shelves where they'll squeeze out. Maybe they'll pretend that they were looking for someone and then leave.

They came in because the soft purples and yellows of this place looked comforting and familiar. It's a little crowded, but no one is looking at them funny.

Most people in line with them are staring up at the menu or at their phones. There's even another robot in line, although it looks significantly more human. It's accompanied by a gorgeous woman with thick, curly, white hair that falls down her back and vinyl pants that look like she waded through an oil spill.

She orders for them, and then the two sit at the window together. It looks oddly romantic, with her pulling out the chairs for both of them and the robot affectionately leaning against her side.

"Next?"

Purcell jolts back into their body at the barista's voice. They forgot to leave the line while watching the—Yep, definitely a couple. They flush watching the robot press a sweet kiss to the woman's temple with their damned silicon lips that actually *move* and can probably *feel*.

"Hello?" The barista calls again, and Purcell lurches forward to exit the line.

"I'm so sorry. I wasn't paying attention and—"

"Oh, don't worry, hon. What would you like?" The barista, Lorena, asks, and Purcell gapes at her for a solid second before looking up at the menu.

"Um… I can't… drink, I'm pretty sure. I don't even know where it would go if I'm being honest."

Lorena laughs while Purcell tries not to spontaneously combust. That's probably a thing that they can literally do now, with their luck.

"I just came in here because… it looked nice. It feels good. I don't know," they explain weakly.

"Well… Can you smell?"

"Uh, no," Purcell mumbles once it hits them what they were missing.

"I'll give you a regular latte then. It's free."

"Free?" They gasp. They completely forgot that they don't have money.

"Yeah, hon. It's Condition 3," Lorena explains with that same sweet smile. She looks tired, but it seems genuine. "What's the name for your order?"

"Purcell."

"For here?"

"Please."

"Okay. We'll call your name."

"Thank you." They rush away to find an empty table in the back of the café.

They choose an armchair in front of a bookshelf and a successfully-nosy distance away from a chess set if someone starts playing. They can just barely spot the human-robot couple through the line of people.

No one else is looking at them, but not in an uncomfortably-not-looking way, in a we-see-this-all-the-time way.

"Purcell?" Lorena leans over the side of the counter to set a tray down. She didn't put it with the rest of the orders on the opposite side of the café, which Purcell is thankful for because they didn't have to navigate through the crowd to grab their drink.

"Thank you so much," they whisper before scooping up the tray and returning to their chair.

When they sit down, they see the latte art decorating the mug. It even hangs off the side in some places where the foam is thickest.

It's a panda. One of the baristas created a little foam, latte art panda for them.

If they could cry, they're sure that they would.

Instead, Purcell clutches their mug close to their chest and stares in awe at the cute, foam creature. Its head pokes out of the latte in a white dome decorated with dot markings and a smile. It has two nubs for its paws, where they rest over the rim of the mug. The features are lopsided because whoever drew them made one eye droopier than the other, and one ear is lower than the other. They want to take a photo of it, but they can't.

Their left hand twitches, and the panda's arms detach from its body as the coffee sloshes around.

Purcell puts the mug on the table before they can destroy it more, and they watch as their twitchy arm spasms.

They distract themselves with one of the books behind them and grab one titled *Robot Matters* with a gray, mechanical heart stitched onto a black cover. They skim the table of contents for anything interesting. 'Foreword, Introduction, 2050 to 2080, The Robot Wars, Postwar-2085, Future Predictions, Why Work Together?, Conclusion,' with a publication date of 2086, makes Purcell understand that they're holding some kind of political manifesto from 14 years ago.

They flip through and skim a lot of it, long enough that when they check on their panda friend, it's mostly dissolved into an unrecognizable blob. The dots where its eyes and ears were are still visible, so it looks more like a domino tile.

When they turn to put the book back, their wrist twitches wildly before their fingers all straighten out against their will. The book falls, and they have to lean sideways to reach it with their opposite hand before putting it away.

Purcell pokes at their hand to try to find the magic wire that will fix them. Certain places burn significantly to touch. The trial-and-error (and it's only errors) makes them give up. They're not fixing anything anytime soon on their own.

They think to go look for a mechanic, but they want to return their latte with some kind of thank you. It feels wrong that they can come in and order something without paying. They can't even show their appreciation by drinking it. They should buy a notebook and pen so they can write a *Thank you!* next time.

They have a harder time carrying the tray back to the counter because of their unbending fingers.

"Thank you for the panda. It was very cute," they mumble

and prepare to turn and run.

They weren't even sure any staff member heard them before Lorena smiles and thanks them.

"Yeah. Thanks. Bye." Purcell scrambles out of the café and chooses a direction to walk at random.

There are often groups of people walking or standing around together, but they aren't talking. There are also plenty of groups all speaking, but it's the silent ones that they find odd. They walk behind a large group of teenagers for a while that are all silent aside from the occasional laugh, but they're also all looking at each other, nodding, reacting to things together.

It takes Purcell several minutes to notice that they all have earbuds in. They must be able to hear each other somehow.

Purcell also passes a few people in formal work clothes. One is gesturing widely as he assumedly is speaking because the others nod and follow along, but it's silent. His mouth isn't even moving.

They resolve to look it up later. They thought they would stumble upon a mechanic naturally, but most shops in this area are insurance firms and financial businesses. There are plenty of vague tech companies around, but nothing with the feel of a mechanic that can fix them.

They turn a corner into a gross alleyway to try to find the grimier locations.

After a few minutes of following the most questionable streets, Purcell finds a 'Repair Store'. It has large, pixelated posters of phones, laptops, and robots in the windows.

They enter despite the weird vibe it gives them. It feels like they're voluntarily walking in to get a vaccine out of a van in a parking lot. The fact that repair shops are their equivalent to a doctor now really creeps them out. They didn't even trust most of their doctors. How on earth are they supposed to trust someone who thinks that they're just a machine?

Purcell looks through the shelves as they wonder all of this. It luckily isn't too uncomfortable in here. There's a lot of open space, and the surfaces are wiped clean.

The man at the cash register is reading a book and barely glanced at them when they walked in.

They stand at the end of an aisle so they can read all the signs in front of the register without getting close enough that he starts talking to them. One of the sheets says, 'Please have your robots R-# visible or written down,' which they don't love to see.

There's another that's even worse. 'Robots without sentience need to be accompanied by an owner.'

They have sentience, right? Isn't that what Crystal's mom had been saying? Purcell steels themselves before walking to the front.

"Hi," they greet him quietly.

He sets down his copy of 'Midas Touch: The Chrome Age Guide to Financial Dominance' and smiles in a way that looks like *Get on with it.*

They show him their stiff hand, and his brows shoot up. "Wow. That's bad. Has someone looked at this already?" He leans forward as if to poke at their exposed wires, and they pull their hand back.

"No," they answer harsher than they should. They remind themselves that they need this man to want to help them and take a deep breath before explaining. "No, I tried to fix it myself, but…" They wave it around to show that it's obviously still broken.

"Right. It might just be your model. Why are you in that one anyway? Haven't gotten an upgrade?"

"I don't know. No." They watch him type in PRL-5370. "Are you new? You're not in our system."

"Yeah. I am."

"That's fine. Here, fill this out."

Purcell takes the paper and a pen to start filling out the form on the glass counter beside him. He picks his book back up as he waits.

They get stuck early on. They have their name, birthday, residence, and R-#, but no proof of sentience. There's space for another seven-digit number.

"Uh…" They start and wait for him to look up. "What do I put here? For sentience."

The man frowns and waits as if they'll have a better, second question lined up. "What do you mean? You don't have a form for it?"

"No?"

"You haven't done a court case?"

"No."

"Were you created with it?"

"Um… I think, yeah. Probably, that's right, I mean."

"Then the person who made you should have registered you. You need to get that number from them."

"Oh. Um… Okay. That'll take a while probably." They pass the half-finished form back to him.

"Sorry 'bout that. If it's easier, you can come in with a friend— a human one. They can sign for you. But I'm not allowed to operate on an unclaimed bot."

Purcell sighs and clenches their fist to not argue. "Cool. Great. Thanks for your help." They turn on their heel to leave.

The man laughs under his breath as they exit his store.

Chapter 6

It's only when they're walking across the bridge do they remember that they still don't have any money here. It's probably a good thing that man turned them away, or else they would've had a different, just as embarrassing encounter if he had asked them to pay after fixing their wrist.

It's easy to find Tallis's shed following the dirt road. It's the only building in this area not completely absorbed by plants—only mostly.

Purcell bangs their good hand (although they'd argue this metal limb is just as bad) against a metal panel. The wall rattles loudly. It sounds like the place is getting attacked.

"Hello?" Tallis's voice calls from deep inside the building.

The garage door is closed, so Purcell walks through the actual door.

"Oh! You're back!" He sounds happy to see them.

"Yeah, whatever. I need your help." They wave their stiff hand around, and his brows furrow.

"Is it stuck? Oh, wow. It *really* is. Go ahead and sit." He waves at the evil chair in the center of the floor. There's a workbench wheeled beside it that makes it look a little less disconnected, but it still gives them the creeps.

"I'd rather stand."

"Huh?" He looks over his shoulder from where he's grabbing tools to see them standing there, clutching at themselves like a lost child. "Okay. No worries." He sets his tools down on a stool with wheels and pulls it with him as he gets closer.

Purcell goes very still as he waits for them to offer their hand again. They stare at him and remember being ripped away from their home and out of their body.

"Are you ready?" he asks, but all they hear is him telling them that their life isn't real.

"No."

"Okay." He waits.

After a couple of minutes, Purcell uncrosses their arms and extends their broken one to him.

He reaches to hold it, but pauses and waits for their confirmation again. They wish he was less considerate. It would make it easier to hate him.

Tallis wraps his large fingers around the back of their forearm and inspects the wires coming out of their wrist. He winces, pulls air through his teeth, and gives them a concerned look.

"Has it been hurting you?"

Purcell shrugs, but an internal part of them really wants someone to know that they've been in pain. Even though this man effectively killed them, they know he'll be compassionate because he knows enough about them.

"Only today… when my hand touches anything."

He nods like he suspected as much.

They watch him work. He starts by opening a panel in their upper arm and disconnecting something, which makes their whole arm go limp. They can't feel anything as he organizes their wires, lays them flat, or tucks them into place. Then he closes their metal shell that contains it all.

He works in near-silence, broken up by little mumbles and hums as he thinks.

They're glad he doesn't ask what happened. They miss the rings they would fidget with, especially their lucky one they'd always wear on their middle finger. Maybe it's a good thing they can't feel anything because the absence of it from their finger would be bothering them even more.

After a certain point, it must all be muscle memory because Tallis works faster and with less commentary.

He reconnects their sensation and gives them a hopeful look as the panel in their upper arm shuts.

"Am I meant to see if it still hurts?" they ask and immediately pat their fingers against their good palm.

"Whoa! Slower!" Tallis panics and reaches for them but stops when they don't flinch. There's only the dull clanking of their hands.

"Good job," Purcell says out of habit and then regrets it when he smiles.

The wrinkles around his eyes look adorable. They're tempted to punch him to see if their hand really is all better.

His soft smile slips back into concern. "Did you find a place to stay? I was worried when you didn't come back last night."

"Did you stay here all night?" they ask incredulously.

"Um… I mean, yeah. I live here." He gestures back at the darkest wall of the shop.

If they squint, whatever that means (zoom in?), Purcell can make out a loft with curtains up in a makeshift bedroom.

"You live here. Oh my God."

He laughs awkwardly and rubs the back of his neck. "Yeah, it's fine for what I need. If you need a place, there's room for—"

"No. I found something."

He deflates slightly, but nods so they know he believes them.

"Thank you, though. Not that I would—" They cut themselves off. They don't want to be *too* rude to him.

"Yeah. Did you go into the city?" He backs away from them finally, and they only realize then how used to his proximity they had gotten.

Purcell frowns and starts planning an escape from this conversation.

"You don't have to tell me. I was just gonna say, it might be good for you to go to the court up there and ask for a name change. That way, you don't have to sign everything as 5370." He points, and they look down at their arm.

"Yeah... I need my sentience number."

"Oh, yeah, that too. You have to change your name first, though." He nods, then falters when they frown. "What?"

"You don't have it?"

"Um... No? I only have you—found you, I mean!" He raises his hands like they're going to attack him.

Smart man, they think again.

Purcell sighs and starts pacing the cluttered space.

There are little robots in doghouse-like stations all over the floor. The floor itself is mostly clear, but every table has some kind of half-finished project on it.

"I can help you if you want, but I don't have a way of getting into the city that easily. I mean, I could walk, but it takes over two—"

"No, that's okay." They turn to him, but he's putting tools back in their boxes and not looking at them.

He looks fit enough to walk the distance. He looks like a mechanic who could lift the back of a car if he needed to.

Tallis turns around, so Purcell goes back to pacing.

"So I go to court, change my name, and *then* file for sentience?"

Tallis nods.

"But none of the repair shops in the city will work on me if I don't have that damn number." They don't know if that's exactly true, but they don't have the energy to try asking around for one either. Besides, a sketchy business model is probably the very last thing that they need.

"Yeah, I'm sorry." He winces and steps closer. "What happened anyway? Can it be avoided for a while? I hate that you have to walk all this way to get... help."

They don't like his pause—not sure what he's thinking. That combined with him getting closer and not wanting to admit that they stress-picked their own wires out of their arm makes them feel like a trapped animal.

They start leaning for the door, ready to run again.

"Wait! Before you go!" He motions for them to stop, and they do. "This was the only thing with you when I found you. I forgot all about it. It was taped to your back." He grabs a severely water-stained folder with elephants on it. It was tucked beside the ominous chair.

Seeing it makes their head hurt. Trying to rub the back of their neck to soothe the ache makes it worse when their fingers wrap around skeletal shafts of metal instead.

Purcell groans and closes their eyes again, which does nothing, so they take the folder and cover their face with it. They sigh in relief when their vision goes black. The elephant-patterned folder blocks their camera, and they hold still so the disorientation will go away.

"Are you alright? Did you remember something?" Tallis's voice sounds the same distance away thankfully.

"I remembered that you're a bitch," Purcell grumbles. They thump their face a few times, but stop after getting vertigo from their vision flashing in and out.

"Are you okay to walk home? Can I give you my number so you can text me when you get there safe?"

"Sure." They discovered the ability to text from their provided computer in their apartment, so they can actually contact him.

"You can always ask me for advice on more minor repairs too. Or look them up, I guess, but there's a lot of people with… conflicting advice. And not all of them know what they're—"

"I will." They cut him off and move the folder.

He returns to their side with a sheet of paper with his number scrawled on it.

They open the folder, he tucks the paper into a pocket, and they snap it shut before reading anything else in it.

"Thanks. I'll be going now." They don't leave any room in their tone for arguing.

"Okay. Be safe."

"I will."

Chapter 7

The sun sets while Purcell walks home. They stop briefly on the bridge to watch the river underneath continue well past the horizon line, so the sun seems to melt into the water.

The purple, pinks, and blues soothe their nerves that are still buzzing after seeing the folder.

As they walk, they enjoy watching the sky darken in the building's reflections.

There's a shiny look to the grass the closer they get to their apartment. At first, they think it's tinsel or something, but there's just too much of it everywhere.

Finally, their curiosity gets the best of them. They look around to make sure no one is watching them before crouching down to inspect the grass.

It's wet. Why is the grass wet?

Purcell pats the springy grass several times and watches in awe as it leaves a pattern of their hand where the moisture lifts. They've never noticed that humidity rests on the grass before. It's so simply beautiful.

"Hey, there's one!" someone yells from down the street.

Purcell looks up to see a group of kids all pointing at them.

"Um…" Before they can say *What?* one of them throws an empty can at them.

It hits a tree and bounces back toward the group, but Purcell panics and stands.

"Ew. Why does it look like that?" another kid yells and makes the others laugh.

"Who cares. I wanna see what's inside that screen head!" One of the larger kids runs at them.

Purcell lurches back and is in the middle of turning when one of them stomps on their knee. They yelp and crumple down.

They hug their folder to their chest as the kids surround them and start kicking and hitting them with random things.

"God, there's not even any give to them. Why is it like that?"

"Do you think it's easier to break this way?"

"It seems pretty—Ugh!" One of them loses their footing after Purcell gets a foot under them to stand.

They watch him catch himself and skid on the sidewalk before they take off.

"It's a runner!" A few of them cheer, but Purcell turns to look back before making their escape.

"The fuck is wrong with you!?" They take a few precious seconds to memorize their faces. It's a group of two girls and three boys, all between 13 and 20 years old probably.

"Oh, is it a person?" one of the girls asks the other.

"It doesn't look like one," one of the guys argues and tenses up to attack again.

"What's going on here?" a much older voice joins in.

It's a cop, stepping out of his car parked right beside them.

"Oh, shit!" Some of the kids shrink back into the shadows.

"It tried to break my fuckin' arm!" the boy who fell points at them, and the officer glares at everyone.

Purcell's heart stops when the cop grabs something off his

belt and points it at them.

The kids gasp in time with Purcell scrambling backward, but then the gun-like machine beeps.

The cop reads whatever it scanned. "It doesn't have sentience. 'S owned by some old lady. It didn't do anythin' to you kids." The man starts to lecture the group. "Let the poor thing go. Did y'all attack it? You know, *you* look familiar, young man." He points, and more kids shrink away into the alley while they still can.

Purcell turns and runs.

They don't get tired, so it's easy to just keep going and going. They run until they feel safe enough to walk alone again.

It takes a long time to find the streets they recognize, and then to cautiously make their way back home. They make many paranoid, intentional wrong turns just in case they're being followed.

The second they lock their front door, they toss the folder onto the counter and lie on the floor.

Their body doesn't hurt exactly, but something is wrong with it. Their balance is off, and some panels on their legs are wiggling when they weren't before.

Purcell stares at the ceiling for several minutes. Their mind wanders from the police officer to being called property to Tallis to... Tallis!

They lurch up and rush to turn on the computer. They drum their fingers impatiently as it loads, and then dig out the slip of paper from him.

'Sorry for the delay. Had to take a bit of a detour. I'm home safe. Please sleep well. —Purcell.' They hit send and fall to lie back on the floor.

They wonder if they should tell him about the scanner that

the cop had. They're glad it didn't have Tallis's information. But then, who is that old woman who came up?

Purcell turns to stare at the folder resting on the kitchen counter. They hope it has something in it for how to get back into their old life. They're tired of living here.

They pick themselves up off the floor, more and more aware of a screechy, grinding sound coming from their hips, and grab the folder.

They sit at their desk to go through the papers one by one. Most of them are warped and water-stained.

After going through them all and gleaning small bits of information from the rare, intact words, they think they understand.

First, they were purchased by a Jasmine M. Bell in 2079 as a Personal Robot of Labor—specifically a caretaker for Miss Bell in her old age. They worked for her until her death on June 12, 2082. Then, per Miss Bell's will, her PRL was put under in a long-term simulation instead of being wiped and re-distributed.

One of the papers is a certificate of purchase for the simulation that they were placed in. It was chosen by Miss Bell because her PRL had apparently shown interest in her piano while working as her hospice nurse.

Another sheet of paper is a very damaged request form that the PRL be disposed of without waking it, so that it not wake up only to be thrown away as the model is no longer valuable. The page is stamped at the bottom by a waste removal company that they agreed to the terms and did not turn on the PRL to offline it before taking it.

Purcell stiffly shuffles the papers together and puts them back in the folder that they now recognize as a remnant of

Miss Bell's elephant-loving home.

Their head aches from all the flashes of images they're receiving—elephant figures on glass shelves, beaded reading glasses, pill organizers, an old wooden piano with yellowed keys.

They try to rub their eyes and instead discover their screen is broken when it makes a crunching noise.

"Shit," they hiss and examine the shards of glass in their hand. They're so small; they look like sand. Tallis will have to fix them again tomorrow.

Purcell sighs and throws their head back to look at the ceiling. It's hard to talk to him without calling him a murderer. Maybe they can convince him to put them back under.

"Do I even believe this?" They mutter to themselves as they go throw away the glass pieces. They're still hopeful that this has all been some elaborate nightmare.

They miss their kind-of-shitty house and their cute, red car, and their corded earbuds. They miss smelling their coffee in the morning and sitting at their piano deciding what to practice.

"God, my piano," they sob into their knees as they crouch in front of the trash can. "I miss my piano." They sound like a petulant child, but it makes them feel better.

The glass clinks at the bottom of the bin, and they push themselves to stand.

If what those papers said is true, they were asleep—or, in their simulation—for eighteen years.

They want to wrap up in their favorite blanket and curl up into a ball on their couch to watch TV. It occurs to them then that the cliffhanger they just left off on might not exist as a show here at all. They don't even try to look it up. They can't take another disappointment today if the show isn't real.

Maybe blankets count as Condition 3. Surely if a latte can be free, then a single blanket should be allowed. Although they have a feeling that the latte art was just to be nice because they saw it listed on the menu on the way out, and it was not supposed to be free. So, maybe they need to find a really nice blanket vendor.

They snort at the thought and rub their face, flinching when more glass falls into their hand. They sigh and throw away more of the little shards.

Purcell didn't sleep last night, and they wonder if they should try again. Exhaustion is slowing their movements and pulling around their face. Usually, they would splash their face with water. They'd probably short-circuit if they did that now.

Maybe they would wake up back home if they died here.

The idea shocks Purcell into moving. They find themselves cleaning up just to have something to do.

There's barely anything in this apartment, so they return to the elephant folder after running out of cobwebs to occupy themselves with. They flip through the papers again, double-checking that they interpreted it all correctly. Even though most of the text is obscured, just holding the pages seems to tell them what they are. It feels like instinctively knowing someone's name in a dream, even if they look completely different.

Purcell blinks at a strange sensation after flipping a page. It's sticking to their hand.

They straighten their fingers and shake it, but the paper stays glued to their palm. Finally, they peel it off with their other hand and frown at the lack of adhesive.

"What on earth...?" Maybe this *is* their dream world. It

certainly feels fake, especially after that oddly pretty water in the grass earlier.

They decide to look it up because they're pretty sure they'd have another sleepless night of staring at the ceiling.

"Actually, let me…" They look that up first.

'Do robots need sleep?' gives too many conflicting answers, so they refine it to PRLs specifically.

'PRL models did not need to be charged because of their solar panels. This type of charging has become obsolete as more robots prefer to wear clothes that would obstruct the panels. More recent models come with a charging cable that requires 240V for 2-4 hours most commonly, although some robots prefer to charge more like a human sleeps with 120V for 6-8 hours. The exception to this is the IRL, which requires 400V for…'

Purcell stops reading. It hadn't occurred to them that they're essentially naked. They can't feel their body, so the lack of clothing isn't very noticeable. The other robots they've seen were wearing clothes, but they also looked more human-like.

They think back to the couple in the café with Lorena and flush at the memory of the robot wearing a sundress that she'd fidgeted with in line, swaying the fabric back and forth against her partner's soft, silicon legs.

The wall in front of Purcell lights up pink as their screen reflects their feelings, and they groan and cover their face. They're not thrilled that they have a non-existent poker face now.

A spiderweb-like pattern of much brighter pink stands out where their screen is cracked. They huff and ignore it to look up the sparkly grass phenomenon instead.

It's called dew apparently. Purcell has heard that word before to describe eyes, like in a cheesy poem, but had never seen the grass shine until tonight.

One mystery solved. They have a harder time finding the answer for the paper sticking to them until they change 'stuck to hand' to 'stuck to metal'.

The answer is static—another thing they had heard of but never experienced before.

They flinch at an abrupt memory of Miss Bell saying she hates fuzzy socks because of static. The old woman had been pouring tea with shaky, knobby hands while Purcell supervised her in the kitchen. It was near Christmas time, and she had told them to take any fuzzy socks that they wanted because she didn't like them but always received them from well-meaning friends.

They remember their chest warming when she patted their hand as she leaned on her walker to get by. They hadn't been sure whether they were feeling love or not. All they knew was that Miss Bell treated them as kindly as if they were her own grandchild.

The memory loops on itself because Purcell can't remember what happened next. Probably watching TV or preparing her a bath.

They pace as they plan what to do for the rest of the night. They'd really like to go for a walk, but they're scared to go out while it's dark now. They'll head to Tallis's the second the sun rises. Even after looking it up, they're not certain that static is normal for this body or if they're damaged and going to be zapping everything they touch.

They'd also like to stop rattling ominously with each step. They sit down partly for silence, partly to stop further scraping their hip joint, and partly to search, 'Why do kids attack robots?'

Many news stories appear about damaged property. It seems common for non-sentient robots to be attacked. Unfortunately, this gives them a new problem. 'How to know if a robot has sentience?'

Most results are blogs describing human-like robots, clothes, and mannerisms, but one is a government website.

> *'innovation.energy.gov*
> *U.S. Department of Energy—Bureau of Robotics'*

It leads to a form for filing for sentience and describes the many tests that robots have to pass. It's very vague about the whole operation, only listing the forms to bring and not the test itself.

They can't save files on this technically public computer, so they go to write the URL down and then sigh when they remember they don't have a pen.

It's a minor inconvenience, but it's enough.

They turn the computer off before lying on the still-bare mattress. They know now that they can't sleep, but they try to anyway.

Besides, watching the dark room gradually fill with color as sunlight peeks through the blinds isn't so bad.

Chapter 8

"I'm not assimilating into the fucking tin man!"

Tallis clenches his jaw but doesn't yell in return. "I just want you to be happy here too."

Purcell sighs, which they discovered is a valve on their ribcage that hisses to release hot air. They drop their head back to look at the metal ceiling.

Their whole torso is even more numb than usual as Tallis adds a feature to them. He already fixed all the damage. They didn't say a word about the group of teens attacking them last night, but he mumbled about ways to improve their design and make them visibly sentient anyway. And now they're in this damn chair again.

Their screen was the most tedious thing to work on. At first, he tried to fit a new one in, but it wasn't the right size, so instead he painstakingly filled every crack in the glass with a special glue. It hardened into a seamless face, but he warned them that it would be more fragile.

Now he's doing something that he didn't fully explain, and the uncertainty makes them jittery. Except, they can't move.

"What are you even doing? Does it really require me to be completely numb?" they ask more directly.

Tallis grunts and keeps gluing a foam-like layer under their metal-shell skin. "I'm making your skin more… just, more. You should be able to feel it… Almost done…" He zones out again.

"What's the point of all this if I'm not even a person?"

"You don't need to be human to be a person," he argues.

"You know what I mean. Why the upgrades? Why fix me at all?"

"I want to," he admits plainly and glances up at their face. "It… pleases me."

"And so you don't care how I feel? It *displeases* me."

He sighs and stops what he's doing for a moment to clench his fists in his lap. "I do care, but I also don't trust your judgment."

They scoff and wish they could move, but they're immobile. "What about *your* judgment? When would you ever believe me about what I need?"

"When you can tell me you don't want this." He points to the project he's partway through, and they can't find it within themselves to argue. They want to know what he's doing.

They pay attention to his music instead.

True to his word, he finishes soon after. He claps expectantly after reconnecting their torso's sensation. It almost looks like he's praying with his palms together while he stares at them.

"What did you do?" They hold still, scared to move.

"Touch yourself. I mean—!" He panics and reaches as if to block a punch.

Purcell laughs at him before poking their side. "Oh." It feels real.

They do it again, this time with their whole hand. They feel the pressure, the shape of their fingers, even a vague idea of the cold metal.

"Can you tell the difference? Tell me if it's dialed up too high.

I tried to guess where the normal range would be, but I wasn't sure."

Purcell nods as he rambles. They're more occupied with being able to feel pressure again than they are with congratulating him.

They feel guilty though, when his voice fades into silence.

His sad smile is so forced; it hurts their heart.

"Thank you… Tallis."

His eyes widen, and he abruptly looks away to cut out more of that spongy, foam material. "Yeah, of course. It's only fair."

"'Fair'?"

"Um… since I woke you up."

"Oh." Their good mood wavers, and he can tell, so he raises the foam and points at them.

"Can I keep going?"

"Sure."

They spend the next hour listening to music and the creaking as he works.

"Alright. Try this one?" he says again.

They poke their arm, nod that it feels right for the fourth or fifth time, and he sighs in relief.

"Great. Well, I'm hungry, so…" He wipes his hands and peels some glue off his fingers while walking to the beat-up fridge in the back. "Sorry I couldn't fix your thinnest bits yet. I'll need to get you a different skeleton before adding stuff to it," he yells over his shoulder.

Purcell nods, and it takes them a second to remember to verbalize it. "Yeah, that's fine."

"Okay." He's mumbling around food now, and they get up to see what it is.

He's making a sandwich and munching on plain slices of

cheese as he does.

"You're so weird," they tease, and he jumps at their voice so close.

"Hm?" He raises an eyebrow and chews cutely, like a chipmunk.

"Nothing." Purcell backs away and looks around one last time.

One of the little, one-wheeled robots is out today. It acts like a dog—wheeling around the garage and beeping at random things. They're not sure it even does anything useful.

Tallis affectionately patted its head when it rolled up to them earlier. It had beeped a bunch and then left.

It's purple wheels make them think of the café.

"Well, this has been fun. I'm gonna head out." They make the mistake of looking at Tallis after their announcement and feel a sharp pang in their chest.

He nervously glances at them, grabs his plate, and rushes over to catch them before they can leave. He's a grown ass man. He should not make them think of a puppy.

"Are you really okay? I can always go with you. It's not like I'm actually trapped over here." He sounds surprised by his offer too.

"No, I am. Yesterday was… an outlier."

"What happened?" he asks for the first time and anxiously reaches for them.

They give him their hand by reflex since he held it earlier to buff scuffs out. His thumb rubs where the scratches used to be.

"Just some dumb kids. Thought I was a gardener bot or somethin'. I don't know."

He sighs and rubs his thumb over their name, PRL-5370. "I'm sorry…" He looks up.

It doesn't quite register as eye contact because their camera is higher than their screen face.

"A few more upgrades and most people should be able to tell that you're a person."

"It's stupid that that's needed at all," they argue again, like when this topic first came up. "I don't like to have to constantly think about how my dumb, little robot-self can mimic what *I had!*"

"Let me do it then," he offers.

They wish they could faze him with their yelling, but they never do. "Let you do the thinking?" they repeat and can't help but glare at him.

"No. Well, kinda, but no. Let me worry about the next upgrades. Unless something really specific comes to mind, don't worry about knowing what to… order? Ask for?"

They mull it over. It doesn't sound so bad, although they don't like relying on others to fix them. "I wasn't overly fond of being in the dark while you took me apart."

Tallis blinks, shocked that it hadn't occurred to him. "Oh, I'm sorry. You can always yell at me when that happens."

"Yeah, you seem to enjoy it anyway." They meant it to come out teasing, but it sounds factual.

They both freeze for a second too long to go unnoticed before he laughs it off.

"I think you've earned the right to yell at me a bit. I'm sorry I couldn't ask before waking you up. It didn't seem… I didn't think you would be…"

"Upset?"

"No, I mean, yeah but—I didn't think you were in there as long as you were. Like I said, you were in such great condition; I thought a museum threw you out to be honest."

"Hm."

There's an awkward silence that they both work to ignore.

Purcell flinches when they remember another question they had.

He jumps after they do and watches them closely for what their thinking.

"I had this weird… phenomenon happen. And I wasn't sure if it was normal or safe or… anything. I looked it up but…"

"Yeah?" He starts rolling one of the chrome beads in their knuckles with his thumb.

"Is static normal? A paper was stuck to my hand for a while, and I had to peel it off. I was worried I was gonna zap people or something."

"Oh… It kind of depends."

They wait for him to explain.

"A little bit of static is fine, but if it's ever visible, then it's bad."

"Like the paper?"

"No, I mean… the electricity can build up. It'll look like tiny lightning, like… white sparks. That's bad."

"Oh. I didn't see any."

"Then you should be okay."

"Okay…" They want to ask him about dew as well, but hold it in for now. That seemed normal after looking it up. Plus, imagining it makes them think about the attack.

Tallis drops their hand to eat, and Purcell brushes their fingertips together a few times. They look forward to being able to feel everywhere, despite how each upgrade cements the possibility that their whole life really was a simulation.

They sigh and turn to leave.

"Be safe! Text me when you can."

"Yeah. Thanks again."

They both wave, and then Purcell walks to the café.

They arrive around the same time as before, and something in their chest starts whirring when they see Lorena at the register.

They get in line and hope she'll recognize them. She probably will, right? They have yet to see another robot that looks like them.

"Purcell! How are you?" She greets them with a bright smile despite the bags under her eyes.

"Hello. I'm doing well actually. How are you?"

"'Actually'? That doesn't sound good."

Purcell winces, but she's nice enough to not point it out.

"I'm doing good too, thank you! Do you want another latte?"

"Yes, please."

"Coming right up, honey."

"Thank you." They head for their chair from last time, but an old man is sitting there, talking and smiling with his wife while they watch TV in the corner.

Purcell pivots and looks for the next best chair, which happens to be the only empty one. They claim the stool beside the counter and watch as Lorena's coworker trades to take orders so she can make drinks.

They watch Lorena turn on a really loud machine and do something with a silver pitcher for a long time. Her back is to them, so they stare without feeling creepy. They also have a view of a single, yellow butterfly clip about to fall out of her hair.

Lorena has straight black hair that doesn't quite reach her shoulders. She's fairly short, having to reach up for most things on the counter, and is wearing a boxy dress that matches her apron. She looks comfortable and friendly, like a character in a children's book.

Purcell looks to the registers when she turns around, but then smiles when she sets the mug in front of them.

"Ta-da! One cute bear for my cutest customer!"

Purcell sputters, which they can now feel as the valves on their sides flutter wildly. "Oh, gosh, I uh—Thank you." They pull the mug closer and "Aww" at the art.

It's a polar bear made out of foam and drops of chocolate sauce.

"Incredible."

"Thanks, hon! Enjoy! Oh, I mean—"

They both laugh it off, but it sends a jealous pang through their chest. They commit to memory to look up 'Can robots drink?' later.

Purcell doesn't stay in the café as long as the first time. They don't have the books to occupy themselves with, and they feel weird watching the baristas so close.

When there's a break in orders, they wave Lorena over.

"Yes, hon?"

"Your clip is about to fall out."

"Hah?" Her brows furrow, and she pats all over her head like she didn't know something was in her hair. "Oh, shit!" She laughs and looks at the yellow butterfly. "Thank you! That must've been in there all day, *God*!"

Lorena smiles at them, glances at the waiting customer, but then gets waved off by her coworker. She waves back a silent *Thank you* and steps up to the counter to keep talking to Purcell.

"Are you enjoying your bear?"

"I am, thank you."

They both watch the remnants of it float on the coffee.

"Well, a better time than *it's* having," she jokes, and Purcell huffs a laugh. "Also, I'm just curious…"

"Hm?"

"Why are you in such an old model? Surely most people are dicks to you."

"Oh, uh. Yeah." Purcell nods and stalls as they come up with an answer. "I'm working on getting upgraded, but it's taking a long time."

"Oh." Lorena frowns like she has more questions now.

"Yeah, I'm not sure when I'm gonna hit that threshold that… people put it together."

"Mh, that sounds tough." She solemnly nods. There's a strange lull where she stares at them like she's waiting for something, and they hope she isn't wondering if they're not sentient after all.

They adjust on their chair, although they're glad that things can feel uncomfortable again.

"How old are you?" she asks.

"Oh, um…" They blank for a moment but eventually remember their last birthday. They had ordered expensive wine and macarons to snack on while watching soap operas that they unironically enjoy. "29."

Lorena's eyes widen before she cutely blinks with a blank expression.

"What?"

She shakes her head and smiles awkwardly. "I don't know why; I thought you were a lot older for some reason."

"Old model?" they guess.

"Not even that. You just seem…"

"Old?" they tease her, and she starts sputtering.

"Not in a mean way! You seem so calm and collected, like

quiet. You just seem like you should be knitting in a corner and talking shit about the youth or something." She waves toward the chairs in the corner like she's picturing Purcell doing exactly that.

They snort and duck at the weird sound that comes out.

Lorena giggles too, then abruptly squeaks out an apology and leaves to make a drink.

Purcell watches as she rushes to blend ice and stir together something strangely purple before handing it off and returning to them.

"Sorry about that."

"Oh, you're fine. I'm the one distracting you from work."

"And since you're so curious, I'm 25, by the way," she says with more bite than they expected.

"Ah, sorry." They hadn't even thought to ask.

They feel a little guilty and are about to leave when Lorena asks, "What happened to your glass?" She reaches across the counter and lightly rubs the seams that Tallis filled earlier.

Purcell freezes and feels something start whirring in their chest—a fan, maybe.

"Is this stuck? What is it?"

They realize she's trying to clean their face and wonder for the first time what it looks like. "Is it bad? The… mechanic that fixed it said it looked fine," they grumble.

Lorena pulls her hand away, but then shakes out of the focus to reassure them. "Oh, not at all! I didn't even notice it until now. There are just some lines that don't reflect with the rest of your face."

"Oh. He repaired the cracks with plastic, so that makes sense."

"Ah." Lorena cutely nods with her mouth open. Then she frowns and purses her lips when they never answer her original question. "How'd it break?"

"Uh… Like you were saying… those dickhead kids nowadays," they grumble with a fake drawl and look down.

Lorena laughs, then immediately looks guilty. "Sorry. That's awful, but—"

"No, you're okay." They wave it off. They were trying to make her laugh after all. "I think I'm gonna head out now though."

"Oh, alright. If you must!" She uses a fake accent and dramatically throws her head back while laying a hand on her chest.

Purcell does that awful snorting sound again. It sounds like a toy car is backfiring as the valves on their sides sputter.

"God, I need to ask him to fix that noise," they mutter as Lorena smiles at them again.

"No, it's *cute*! Don't get *rid* of it," she begs, but doesn't seem serious.

"We'll see."

"Who can even work on you at this point? I'd be scared if I were you, letting just anybody try and fix me up." Lorena shudders at the thought.

"Yes! Thank you! I'm so glad I'm not the only one who thinks that!" They lean forward and do their best not to get too loud.

Lorena sympathetically pats their shoulder and nods with her lips pressed in a flat line.

"Who though? Because I have recommendations if you don't like yours."

"Really? I might take you up on that," Purcell admits, then winces at her concerned expression.

"Really? Why?"

"Well…" They look around, suddenly paranoid that Tallis is

watching somehow. "He's nice and all, but…" They actually have a hard time coming up with a complaint for a moment. "He does a great job, but he's not the most open. Sometimes he'll start working on me without telling me what he's changing."

"Oh, that's not good." She grimaces, and Purcell nods before continuing.

"And I won't go into much detail, but we met in a… He kind of created some—*most* of the problems that we're having to fix now."

"Hm…" She nods despite looking a little lost, but they don't want to get into the simulation mess right now. "Well, if you ever want an alternative, you let me know, okay?"

"Thank you. I will… He does do a good job though… I should probably be more grateful that he can work on me at all, judging by how old everyone thinks I am." They feel themselves getting too serious, so they veer into teasing Lorena a bit.

She playfully sighs and pats their arm. "Oh, come on. I explained what I meant." There's a thin string of hurt in her words that makes it clear she's taking their teasing more seriously than they intended.

"You did."

They both smile, and Purcell takes advantage of the lull to finally leave like they said.

"Well, thank you for letting me distract you so much."

"Any time, hon." Lorena smiles sweetly and backs away toward the registers. "Be safe!" She yells as Purcell pushes out the door.

"Bye! You too!" They wave back before heading home—*to the apartment*, they correct themselves with a frown.

Purcell huffs and keeps their head down as they walk.

Chapter 9

Halfway through the sleepless night, Purcell starts pacing the connected kitchen and living room. They've run out of patience staring at the ceiling. Never in their life did they think they would miss waking up to their alarm, but they find themselves missing its annoying ringing so they would know they had slept. They want to wake up looking at their familiar ceiling, nestled under the blankets that smell like their house.

They considered going to buy sheets for their bare mattress, but they're still skittish about being out at night.

They spent too much energy researching robots earlier, and now they're feeling claustrophobic in this cold shell all over again.

But worst of all, they want to play piano.

They want to have a slow morning of opening the blinds, stretching their wrists and fingers, scooping coffee grounds, and listening to the music they create by practicing their favorite songs. They want to feel the weight of the pedals under their foot and the solid pressure of the keys under their fingers.

They search for the next best thing.

There's a music store nearby, and they memorize the route to take in the morning. There's also a school that has piano classes, and they search for a long time to see if they offer community lessons, but all the results are inconclusive.

When it's light outside, they go to the music store. It's a small, hole-in-the-wall type of place between a church and a kebab shop.

The employee turns in surprise when the door dings. "Uh, hello?" The kid, maybe a teenager, has a bewildered expression.

"Hey." They ignore him to look around for the keyboards.

"Are you here to pick up?" he asks.

"No, just window-shopping."

"Oh… Okay." He goes back to fidgeting with something behind the front desk.

Purcell circles the store for a minute, skimming boxes of amps and speakers, then stuff for electric guitars, then drums, and then the keyboards.

The ones available to practice on are on stands stacked on the wall like shelves. They pick one at a comfortable height to play while standing and turn it on. They play a C-chord and jump at the high volume.

"Fuck, sorry," they say just loud enough for the employee to hear.

He laughs it off but comes over to watch.

They fight not to get upset, but their warming screen gives them away.

The man watches as they turn the volume down on the keyboard. It isn't like a real piano, where the weighted keys determine the volume with how hard you press.

"You know how to play?"

"In theory…" They set their hands on the keys and play a very wonky few chords.

"First time playing?" He must not know that their red screen means he should be less annoying.

"A keyboard—yes."

He waits.

"I have a piano. *Had* a piano."

"Ah." He nods. "Makes sense. We only carry keyboards, but I can give you a coupon for the Yamaha place down by 485."

"Um… yes, please. Thank you."

"No problem! That sounded good too! And I got a friend who *hates* keyboards 'cause she grew up with a piano. Says they're 'bout as useful as a leaky cleaner bot," he jokes, then falters.

"Mh."

"Sorry, that's probably uh—Anyway." He winces and stiffly hands them a business card.

There's a code on it for 15% off the $1,120,000 grand piano.

The door dings, so he smiles and returns to the desk, and Purcell realizes they can't pocket the piece of paper. They *have* to hold it in their hand.

They briefly consider trying to pry open the compartments on one of their limbs to stash it there, but it might get damaged.

They place it like a sheet of music for now to keep clunking away at the shitty, plastic keys. They've never felt so spoiled by their real piano in their whole life.

Running through their familiar warm-ups is horrifyingly difficult. It must be because they can't really feel their hands. They can only monitor each finger to press exactly the right notes. There's no muscle memory when there are no muscles for them to use.

They fight the urge to cry and keep telling themselves that all they need is their hands to be upgraded, and they'll be as amazing as they remember.

They stay in the music store well past the polite amount of time for only window shopping. They're grateful the staff doesn't check on them again.

He gives them a thumbs-up on their way out, and they wave in thanks with the coupon in their hand. They hadn't considered it until now, but they can't remember how they bought their piano back home.

Purcell freezes on the sidewalk and frowns as they think back. Some impatient people shove past them, so they press against a brick wall as the world spins faster under their dumb, kickstand feet.

How did I afford my piano? They remember seeing it every morning between their kitchen and living room. It was a permanent feature in their life. They can't remember anything at all before... their routine.

Their routine has always been: wake up, coffee, practice, plan performances, watch TV, shower, order food, sleep. The fun days are the performances. Sometimes the venues are nearby, and sometimes Purcell takes the train, but the events are always the same.

They get there early, tour the place, practice, talk and socialize occasionally, perform perfectly, then go home.

The harder they try to remember anything from before their beloved schedule, the more their brain insists and loops the same scenes over and over.

Beeping pulls them out of their head. They turn to see where it's coming from, but it's *them.*

"What? What is..." Purcell pats their shoulders and back of their neck where the high-pitched beeping is coming from, but then it stops.

"Um?" They clutch at their shoulders for a moment. They're

glad the noise stopped, but they wish they'd figured out what it was first.

They watch the morning rush for several minutes. Once they're sure the beeping won't return, they resume their walk to the school.

It's misty today. They're glad Tallis patched their screen because they're sure they would have short-circuited by now.

Something heavy rolls in the back of their mind like a sleeping dragon. Thinking about Tallis brings the muddled applause turning into the storm and the feeling of numbed touches and restraints—the terrible welcome to the real world that he had greeted them with.

They wish they could hurt him for killing them. They want to tear away everything he's ever known and cared about and replace it with the dysphoric existence that they're navigating through. They want to make him feel as cold and isolated and lost as they feel, all because he just *had* to wake them up.

They scowl, and the people on the sidewalk give weird looks and wide berths as they pass.

He probably woke them up so they could become another little bot in his garage like all his other animatronic pets. They bet he's upset that they left because he was hoping to have a new robot worker, devoid of any personality.

They kick at a rock in their path to get some excess energy out, and it skips out of reach.

They huff and focus on the street names to ensure they don't get lost.

When they reach the school, it looks closed. The front door opens, and it's dark before they hear a click and motion-detector fluorescents all illuminate at once.

"One moment and I'll be right with you!" a woman yells from

a room behind the front desk.

"Alright, thank you!" Purcell yells back. They skim the flyers on the tables in the waiting area. The school has a recital soon where their students of all ages will be able to show off what they've been learning.

There's a $42 entrance fee, which would normally be very cheap if they had a job, and it doesn't say anywhere that the event is open to the public.

"Hey, sorry about—Oh." The woman frowns when she sees them. "We don't talk to representatives. You'll have to come in yourself," she says icily and turns on her heel.

"What? Wait! I'm not—What are you saying?" They flail and sigh in relief when she doesn't flat-out ignore them.

"Your owner," she says and looks at them like they're stupid.

"Uh, no? I don't—I'm just me. I'm a person."

She scoffs as she assesses them. "Really? *You're* sentient?"

Their patience wavers at her patronizing tone.

"I know. It's a long story, but yes. I'm working on it." They gesture to their face, and she purses her lips before stepping closer to hear them out.

"Okay… What did you need?"

They hesitate as they decide on how to approach this. They didn't expect to get this far, so they have no plan.

"Um… I'm trying to practice piano. I've played for years but recently moved and uh… yeah. I guess, are your pianos open to the public or—"

"No."

"Oh, okay. Um…" They expect her to offer alternatives, but she seems resigned to say as little as possible in the hopes that they'll go away.

"Are you accepting new students? Can I enroll?"

The lady sighs and turns her back to them to flip through a filing cabinet. She turns with a manila folder and slides it over to them.

"Fill this out. You can scan it and email it to us. The address is in there. Or bring it back in person, and whoever is working will help you out."

"O-oh. Thank you." They skim the first page and frown at the dreaded 'Proof of Sentience' space that they were hoping not to see. "Could I start here while my sentience case is still being finalized or—"

"No. If you can't fill out the form correctly, you can't be a student here." The woman huffs at them, and Purcell resolves to leave before they lose their temper.

"Okay. Great. Thanks so much for your help," they grumble as they close the folder and walk out.

"You're welcome," she shoots back and scoffs at their rudeness while also turning away.

Purcell stomps out of the building, wishing they could report her for prejudice or something. They doubt anyone would take them seriously.

As they walk back to their disgusting apartment, the ever-present mist transforms into proper rainfall. They hold the folder parallel to the ground so the water drops ideally won't reach the papers inside.

They walk slowly and hunch over a bit to block rain that way too, and they blink in surprise at the light drumming sensation on their shoulders.

They can feel the rain.

Purcell expects the prickly feeling of their eyes watering, but nothing happens. They let the dullness wash over their mood to fully submerge themselves in crying. It doesn't work.

They enter their apartment long enough to drop the folder on the counter before turning right back around to go outside. They have a specific upgrade to request.

Chapter 10

"You want to be able to eat and to cry?"

"Yes." They nod. "Or drink at the very least. It's disconcerting not being able to drink water anymore." They're hoping to distract him from the stranger request by talking about the first.

Tallis nods and spaces out. He fidgets with a tool they don't know the name of and stays silent for a long time.

"So…" they break. "Can you do it?"

He jumps and rushes to reassure them. "Yeah! Sorry. I'm thinking of the best way to… I can do a temporary fix fast and then properly upgrade you after some more… parts arrive, or…" He scratches at his dark half-stubble, half-beard. "It shouldn't be too big of a hurdle to do the vacuole first and then replace it later…"

He nods and focuses back on them. "Yeah. I think I can do that now." He claps his hands and gestures for them to sit.

"Okay, cool." They plop down on the evil chair, almost giddy this time.

They frown at their own enthusiasm and watch as he digs through a bin of junk. He lays some weird tarp bags on the table beside them before grabbing familiar tools from his usual toolbox.

Their good mood fractures into anxiety as he prepares to work on them.

Tallis is silent as usual as he works, so they only have the rain to listen to. This upgrade takes less time than their skin did, and he's putting them back together just as they're starting to get bored.

"Okay. You should be... Well, let me..." He mumbles and reaches for their face.

Purcell glares and grabs his hand. "Tell me what you're doing," they remind him.

"Shit. Sorry, yeah." He steps back and rolls his wrists as he stares at them. "I'm not used to working on *people*. I'm sorry," he repeats. "You have a stomach now. I was going to refix the intake tube to make sure nothing seeps into the non-waterproof parts of you."

"Okay... Is that like... my mouth?" They reach up and pat their flat, mouthless face.

"Yeah. It's here." Tallis brushes something around their neck, but they can't feel it.

"I don't know where you're—" They cut off with a choked, quick inhale through the valves on their sides as he presses his palm flat under their jaw and moves their head a bit. The movement informs them that he's pointing out where their Adam's apple would be if they weren't a metal stick of a robot.

"Does that make sense? I have a mirror in the back, but it's fixed to the wall. I'll show you how this works in a minute."

Purcell nods and daydreams as he rummages around in the equivalent of their esophagus. They catch themselves mentally cataloging the chores they need to do when they get home, then frown when they remember that laundry is not a thing they have anymore.

"Okay. Let's test it out." He backs away and grabs a glass of water before leading them to the back of the shed.

Their eyes instantly adjust to the darkness, and they frown at the feature making itself known.

There's a toolbox back here filled with clothes, a pane mirror attached to the wall, and a surprisingly nice rug and armchair facing the wall.

"You have a thing for watching paint dry?" they joke without thinking.

"Hm?"

They point to the chair.

"Oh." To answer, he flicks a switch on the wall, and suddenly there's a screen where previously there was nothing.

"What? What the hell did—" They gasp when he reaches to stick his fingers through it.

It's lasers. The white loading screen shines on his skin where it hovers in the air.

"Why isn't it projecting on the wall? How is it just—" They wave around.

"Wow. You really *are* old."

Purcell sighs. "This again?"

"'Again'?" He smiles and then explains that the two sets of lasers hit each other to become a makeshift hologram in the air.

"Oh. Are these common?"

"Yeah. It's just a screenless TV. Most people have one."

They huff. *They* don't have one.

Tallis chuckles before steering them back to the mirror.

They thought he had moved on, but he brings up their 'Again' statement during his *How to Eat* presentation.

"I have this… friend."

They start, but get interrupted by his excited "Oh, good!"

"And she was asking about me, of course. Said I was… that I seemed much older."

"Yeah. That's funny. I think you act appropriately for how old you are," he jokes, then blinks in confusion. "Did you tell her about the simulation?"

"No."

His shoulders fall.

"What? Do you want me to go around spreading the fact that you accidentally killed and birthed somebody in 10 seconds?" They bristle and curl their lip up, which they're sure looks ridiculous on the screen.

For some reason, the part he gets hung up on is "10 seconds? It took me 6 months to fix you—to repair everything." He shakes himself out of the strange, defensive feeling. "Sorry, that's not impor—"

"Really?" They're so caught off guard; it feels like their arms hang heavier by their sides.

He doesn't repeat himself, so the two stare blankly at each other until he breaks with, "You don't need to keep that like a secret though. I don't mind you… confiding in people. It's okay."

"I guess you can't be charged with murder if I never existed in the first place."

His eyes widen, and he jerks forward to hold them but stops. When they don't move away, he grabs their shoulder and stares at them with an expression like an open wound.

"*Purcell.*" His face is illuminated by their blue light.

"Hm." Their brain is numbing out, so they cling to his speech.

"Your life wasn't… *false.* It was just… on a detour. You've still been *living.*" He lightly shakes them to reinforce his words.

"Do you think if I died, I would go back home?"

"You don't know that. Don't say things like that," he begs them and clutches a bit tighter.

"If I was certain... I would do it."

His pained gasp hurts as much as their own whispered admittance did.

They close their eyes, but everything stays.

To avoid confronting his concerns, Purcell steps forward and hides their camera against his shoulder. He takes it as a hug, which wasn't their intention, but they can't say it isn't nice.

His arms wrap around their metal shell, and they feel the pressure as the foam underneath compresses. They keep their arms by their side, but push more weight into him in return.

"Thank you," they whisper. The low volume glitches their voice a little, and it comes out with a crackle like an old pair of earbuds.

Tallis rubs their back and whispers, "I'm sorry."

Chapter 11

Legally changing their name took four days, and it was mostly filled with waiting.

Purcell filled out and submitted the forms online, then waited for the reply from the Mecklenburg County Court. They woke up to the 'Confirmation of Name Change' email and headed to Lorena to share the good news.

The café isn't busy for once, and they're as happy to see Lorena as they are worried that she's already working.

"Hi, hon! What can I do for you?" she greets them with a smile, a touch too wide.

"Are you alright?"

"What? Of course." Lorena wavers, and they debate pushing or not.

"Hm... A latte, please... Oh! I can eat now!"

She gasps excitedly, leans forward to joke about something, then falters and frowns at the door behind them.

"Wha—"

"Hon, would you mind turning the sign? It must have flipped in—Sorry. I don't know why I'm asking you. You don't work here." She grumbles to herself as she moves to leave the counter.

Purcell turns to see the 'Closed' sign on the café door.

"Len, it's open," they argue.

"I know, I need to—"

"No, it's—The side facing out says 'Open.'" They grab her as she goes past.

"What? No, it says—" Her eyes widen when it clicks. "Oh." She hides her face in her hands. "God, that's so embarrassing," she mumbles and turns to bump the top of her head against Purcell's chest.

They laugh and hug her, petting her hair until she stands back up straight.

"Are you sure you're alright?" they ask again as she walks back around to the working side.

"Ugh, yeah. Just low on sleep."

"Well… that's really important," they argue.

The milk frother interrupts them as it hisses. Lorena stays silent as she works.

"Here you go." She's dropped the forced, chipper attitude, and Purcell smiles before congratulating her on the wonky latte penguin.

"Very cute."

"Thank you." Lorena slumps against the counter and watches as they tip the mug back to sip their latte. They practiced drinking water in their bathtub for hours until they were sure they wouldn't pour their drink down their front.

They can't taste, but the act of drinking and feeling the weight travel in their torso is familiar enough.

"Thank you." They look to see the damage done to their foam penguin, but it isn't too bad.

"Yummy?"

"Sure."

The two laugh, both aware that Purcell could just as easily be drinking vinegar and wouldn't know the difference.

"Oh, I have good news for you," they remember. "But first—"

"Hm?"

"You're here early. *And* you're tired? What's goin' on?"

Lorena sighs and smiles like she's both annoyed and endeared by the questions. "Thank you for asking. I… Well, I'm covering someone else's shift right now. You know, I'm usually here at 4."

Purcell nods.

"And… First, I want to preface this by saying, I wasn't keeping this from you specifically; I just don't usually… bring it up."

Their brows raise, and they're about to backtrack to tell her not to worry about it when she says, "I have a baby."

Purcell gasps, lurches back, then plants their hands on the counter and leans forward. "That's great! What's their name!?"

Lorena sighs in relief. "Coriander. Corey for short."

"Cute! How old is…"

"She. She just turned 12 months."

"Oh, goodness, that's small. Congratulations!"

She smiles softly and sways like her favorite song has come on.

"Do you have anyone helping you? She must be quite the handful still."

"My mom and step-brother, yeah. They're… helpful."

Purcell chuckles and asks, "Are you sure?"

She inhales slow and deep. "Yes… They're… They're almost *too* helpful. I wish they would…"

"Step back? Are they being overbearing?"

Lorena winces. "*Kind* of? I really appreciate all the time they're spending, but… I don't know. Like, my mom keeps trying to teach Corey bad words and things like that. Funny, 'harmless' things that…"

"That pile up?"

"Yes, exactly." She deflates as they seem to understand.

They take a sip as they think, and Lorena gives them a cute eyesmile.

"What other good news did you have? Are you going to be able to *taste* my coffee soon?" she teases, but keeps a close eye like she's second-guessing if that's polite to say.

"Uh… maybe, but no. I got my name changed!" They sit up straighter and freeze when Lorena falters before cheering with them.

"To Purcell? Or—"

"Yeah," they cut her off in their excitement and display their arm. "It was still legally the—whatever the number is." They twist it to read.

"5370…" Lorena mumbles. "How… cruel."

"'Cruel'?" Purcell's arm flops down to hit their lap with a *clunk* that makes the back of their skull ache. They wince as the reverberations mimic a terrible headache for a moment. Maybe clothes are a good idea.

"Like… I know not every robot is gonna have sentience, but it seems so rude to me not givin' y'all names by default."

"Oh."

Before they can think of a reply, she adds, "I guess it would be impossible to keep track of everyone if they were all just Kates and… I don't know. *Marks*, but—"

They both giggle at her examples, and it breaks her rant.

"It's nice of them to let me name myself before I've even got sentience though."

"You don't have sentience!?" She gasps so loud that a few of the silently working customers look up from their phones.

"Not yet. Not legally. It's a lot longer process, so…"

Lorena is still shaking her head in disbelief.

The conversation pauses so she can take orders, then returns a few minutes later.

"It's ridiculous that they make you do all that. I feel like if I was the judge, you could just walk in and sit down, and I'd know that you're sentient. It's just so *obvious*."

"Yeah? That's good." They feel oddly cold at the reassurance.

"Not that you need to hear that from me," she adds and waves away her previous statement.

Even though her comment stung, Purcell doesn't want her to know, so they quickly add, "I would actually. I *will*, I mean."

She frowns and waits for them to explain.

"Filing for sentience requires two affidavits from sentient beings—at least one human. I was going to ask you and my mechanic."

"Oh!" Lorena's eyes go wide.

They notice for the first time that inside her dark irises are stripes of lighter brown like a latte.

"Do you really want me to do that for you? I feel like you should have someone who knows you better do it, so the court is more—" She cuts herself off when fans turn on around where their heart should be.

Gold light reflects off her glasses as their screen changes color.

"I mean, of course I'd be willing to do it. I'm just… surprised. But I'd love to help you. Especially because, like I said, I know you'll pass." She keeps talking, the longer Purcell is frozen. "Sorry. I didn't mean to ruin your confidence in me. Of course, I'll do my best to write something true and… convincing."

They force themselves to nod. "Thanks, that's uh… good." They release their death grip on the mug to lay their metal palm flat on the counter. "I don't know when I'll do it. Probably soon, but… It might be smarter if I wait for a few more upgrades before trying to convince people I'm a person." They drum their fingers to make a *clink clink clink* sound.

Lorena hums and nods, then has to take an order. She looks annoyed that they've sunken into themselves, but they don't know how to explain how her recommendation hit every weak point in their psyche.

Purcell uses the lull to stare down at their disintegrating penguin and wonder if they should go back into a simulation instead.

Chapter 12

The poster board in the main hallway of their apartment complex has an advertisement for 'Sentient Robots Support Group'. It takes place every Wednesday night in one of the first-floor apartments, and Purcell decides to go.

They're not particularly eager to go to a meeting for a marginalized group that they feel they don't belong to, but it beats staring at the ceiling and rereading the news again. Plus, maybe they'll get lucky and someone there will have advice on filing for sentience or diving into a simulation that feels better than here.

They knock on the door and are greeted by a very humanoid robot in lounge clothes.

Purcell isn't certain if the silicone-covered smiles often don't reach the eyes, but when the stranger tilts their head and asks, "Are you here for the *sentient* robots meeting?" they have a feeling the look is forced.

"Yeah. Is it here?" they ask, even though they already checked twice.

"Oh! Yes, come in, come in! Sorry, we haven't had a new face here in a long time." The other bot motions them in, and Purcell loiters awkwardly in the kitchen with two other similarly human-looking robots, talking over tea.

"Would you like some?" the host offers, but they decline. Everyone here has a working mouth, and they'd rather not become the sad spectacle that can't properly taste. Instead, Purcell resolves to watch as a few more bots arrive—some actually metal like them, with less squishy surfaces.

The host moves everyone into the living room, where the ones who are clearly friends take the couch and leave the rest to sit on the floor around the coffee table.

Purcell wishes they had taken the offered tea just so they could have something to hold and hide behind. They wonder what color their face is and hope it isn't revealing exactly how uncomfortable they feel.

The meeting starts with everyone introducing themselves, and one asks Purcell when they started participating in the Free Body movement.

"The what?" they ask, silently assuming they heard wrong.

"Oh, that's so funny! Have you taken it up yourself? You must be pretty hardcore!"

It sounds like praise, but Purcell just stammers through an introduction that they're new to the city and haven't learned all the group names or trends of anything. The others clearly find them strange, but the group lets them fade into the background as the sharing starts.

Purcell expected to talk about getting attacked in the street for not being human enough. They planned to get assistance in local shops. Hell, they even would have been happy with the others discussing upgrades they want done or recent news stories about IRLs being tested for accidental domestication.

They weren't prepared for a heated discussion on whether or not people can use the word *bot*.

The robot who brought it up is on the couch beside the host, gesturing and talking in a near-human way about how they were personally slighted by their coworker calling them a bot in place of robot. The empathetic nods around the room have to be for show because this is the most unimportant discussion Purcell has ever heard in their life—in both lives!

But then the next topic is on the Free Body movement and how robots should be allowed to dress freely in public, regardless of the model, because nothing about the human-looking ones is unhygienic, so it's safe to be nude and *definitely* not weird.

The next one, the only other screen-faced bot, complains about a recent encounter when a child asked them if they could change their screensaver and how that was an insensitive thing to ask, and that the parents should be ashamed for not teaching him all the proper ways to address people in public.

When everyone but Purcell has gone, they sit in a stunned silence. Then the host jokes that the group shouldn't pressure newcomers into speaking. They all laugh good-naturedly, but some petty spark sends Purcell into bringing up that they want to file for sentience so they can go to school.

There's a pause where the others process the first thing they've said in over an hour, and then the same bot that keeps talking about nudity laws gasps and reaches to touch their arm like they're good friends.

Purcell freezes as they're dragged into a lecture on not succumbing to societal demands and to instead resist the system by not working with the government to legally gain proof of sentience. "The tests are so degrading! They make you jump through all these hoops just to get on the same standing as any human when they should just let everyone pursue whatever they want! It's not right that robots have to prove they're worth the same as any human! It's disgusting!"

"That's not to mention the fact that one of the references has to be human," another adds, and the statement is followed by low groans as everyone reminisces on the process. One of them was created with a sentience certificate, but all the others talk about how long and tedious the process was in order to persuade Purcell to fight to attend classes as they are.

After the fifth, "You'd be such a good movement starter!" they tune everyone out.

The meeting gradually becomes more and more informal as conversations break off into people getting more tea or coming over to tell them how admirable they are for wearing such an old model.

Purcell subtly backs toward the front door to escape and never come back.

While pouring tea, one of the host's friends goes rigid before whirring audibly. They seem to power off.

"Um..."

The screen-faced one follows Purcell's gaze to then flail as they rush over to help their now-offline friend.

"She has an old memory dri—"

"Narcolepsy!" the host yells and waves the first bot away.

The group shuffles her into a corner like they're embarrassed, before the host resets something in the back of her neck that boots her back online.

She laughs it off like it happens often and visibly wilts when everyone keeps treating her like she'll crumble into junk any second.

"Is it serious? Do you need a mechanic to fix it?" Purcell starts to offer Tallis's services when the group flinches at something they said.

"Goodness, you really are rural, aren't you?" one mumbles and forces a laugh to hide their obvious distaste for Purcell. "She doesn't need to be *fixed*. And asking if her disability is serious is awfully—"

"They didn't mean anything by—"

"No, you don't need to argue with them." They cut off the Sleeping Beauty robot like a mother defending a chihuahua with a biting problem.

They keep scolding Purcell for their transgressions as the person that they're defending curls in on herself more and more.

The host glances around with their very human expressions before redirecting the lecturer back to discussing their attempt to publish a book called *We're Not Your Superheroes*.

The bot with the bad memory drive is staring at Purcell like they want to apologize, so they delay their quick escape they could be making.

"Um… about that mechanic," she whispers and smiles awkwardly like she doesn't want to stoop low enough to actually ask Purcell for help.

"Do you want his number?"

"Yes," she whispers even quieter, scanning the room.

"Do you have something to write w—"

"Oh. Just say it. I'll save it into permanent storage," she says, like Purcell is an idiot.

"Into what? Do you have a perfect memory or something? Is that why it's—"

"You don't!?" She gasps and reaches forward like she'll pray for them. It catches the attention of the screen-faced bot, who joins them by the door. "Do you really not have a Cloud server for your data? How do you get anything done?" she whisper-yells, and then Screen-Face also looks at Purcell in shock.

"I don't even know what you're talking about. I either remember shit or I don't. I don't know what to tell you." They shrug, but they really want to start throwing things.

How can these people want to be human so bad while simultaneously taking advantage of inhuman features like manufactured *perfect memory*?

Their face grows hot, and fans kick on in their chest as they reword their defense to have less vulgarity.

"Sorry," she says first. "I didn't realize some robots don't have..." She trails off instead of committing to the apology.

Purcell takes a slow breath before reciting Tallis's phone number without bringing up the numerous conversational black holes they could jump into.

"Thank you. Sorry for... I hope your process for sentience goes smoothly," she whispers and takes a tiny step back so Purcell can excuse themselves.

"Thanks." They nod, accidentally make eye contact with the host, nod goodbye again, and then leave.

Chapter 13

The process of waking up had already been lost in Purcell's previous life, so when they come to in pure darkness with the feeling of sand in their joints, they think they've woken up from a simulation again.

The droning fan noise aligns with the fluttering valves on their sides, so they realize the thing overheating is *them*.

A few seconds pass of muffled noise and feeling like they've died again before their vision returns.

They're standing in their bathroom, facing the mirror after the excruciating self-analysis led them to pick at their appearance for thirty minutes.

Purcell leans to take a step, but the crackling of their ball-bearing joints sends a jolt through their chassis. They yelp and freeze right away.

They try to look down, but the pistons of their neck shutter and cause their head to jerk and stay facing straight. They use the mirror instead to survey all the mindless damage they vaguely remember doing.

Every loose piece of plastic has been peeled and balled up on the counter. Their previously smoothed and oiled joints are all stiff from being prodded at and bent. Every seal in their glass has been torn as they obsessively tried to smooth out every piece of themselves. Their fingers are scratched along with most of the panels that they tried to flatten impossibly flush until the pressure sensors inside their false-flesh buckled.

Shifting their weight creates a terrible vertigo that they think has to do with the sensor they peeled out of the front of their chest. The sticker-like coating had been slightly raised.

Their screen is flickering like they're in turbulence—blue, yellow, black, yellow, blue. The seamless transitions aren't functioning, so they're left with the concentrated hues as their mind races.

They consider stepping into the tub and turning the water on to see what the sparks would feel like, then shake the idea out of their head. Their neck resists all movement, but they find that they can force it if they put enough pressure on it. Unfortunately, the added effort also causes an eerie creaking like a dead tree ready to fall.

For the first time in weeks, they feel a sob escape them.

The catch of the intake hoses on their sides makes them gasp, then cry harder. They can finally feel as their throat lurches and closes up. They feel the shaking of their hands and the weight land in their gut as all the moving parts Tallis fitted them with come into play.

Purcell has never been happier than feeling their breath hiccup like they're still alive.

They don't want to stay in their apartment any longer. The bareness of it was manageable, albeit dispiriting, but seeing pieces of themselves strewn around from their episode makes them want to try to peel themselves out of their metal with more precision.

They're glad they don't own any utensils. They're sure the slippery slope of ridding themselves of every added texture would end with them prying panels off and sawing jagged plastic pieces with a bread knife.

They can't bring themselves to go to Tallis after creating such a mess. They go to the café instead.

Although they almost hope that Lorena isn't working. They want the peace that comes with the place without the confrontation after asking her to write the affidavit.

Still, seeing her through the window as they approach relaxes them.

"I'll be with you in a—Oh, h—Oh my God!"

They laugh under their breath as she cycles through every emotion in five seconds.

"Hey."

"Are you alright?" Lorena stage-whispers as she steps close to examine them. "You look like someone put you through a paper shredder!"

"Thanks."

"Oh, honey. I would hug you, but—" She gestures with the rag she was wiping tables with.

It's then that Purcell sees the baby wrapped to her back. The swaddle blends in with the normally flowy outfits that she wears.

"Is this—! Rosemary? What was it?"

"Corey," Lorena laughs and turns a bit. "Coriander."

Purcell coos and slowly reaches to tap the child's little swaths of black hair.

"Goodness, she's so small!"

"Yep. Just turned 12 months."

"Lovely! But… Why is she here? Or rather, why are *you* here? Is there anything I can do to help?"

Lorena grimaces and glances at the long line that her

coworker is working through. She sighs and turns to face them, blinking hard like she's seeing them again for the first time.

"No offense, hon. But you look close to death. I'd sooner hand you a loaded gun than I would a baby."

"Ah… It isn't *that* bad… Is it?" They look down at themselves and decide that maybe she's right.

They're peeling in every place possible. Things are dented and scratched, if not completely removed. And that's without mentioning their face, which is the worst, with the cracks re-made visible and colors flashing wildly. They should probably have a badge that says 'Caution. May trigger epilepsy' around their neck.

"Well, let me move so you can get in line, but be prepared with your explanation of"—she waves them over—"all this."

"Okay." They do just that—coming up with lie after lie and multiple excuses that they know they won't use.

They briefly consider telling her that her dismissal of their friendship was part of what led them to tear themselves apart like string cheese.

"Christ, not that," Purcell mumbles, and then pointedly ignores the confused look from the patron beside them in line.

Lorena creates the latte art as usual, and Purcell watches, wondering if little Corey should be in here with all these coffee fumes.

"Here you are," she says with a strange tone that makes them frown in confusion. Then they look down to see a butterfly.

"Hm." It's created beautifully, as most of her art is, but they're not sure they like this added visual of how she thinks of them. They feel more like the goop between caterpillar and butterfly at the moment.

"So," Purcell sighs. "Do you want the lead-up or just the crash?"

"Um… lead up?"

"Okay." They stall by sipping their latte and wincing as the too-hot liquid heats up their plastic esophagus. The bag that is their stomach causes fans to turn on as it heats up too, except they sound clipped and create a clicky whirring as they spin.

Lorena glances down at where the noise is coming from before, "Is there any part of you that's working properly?" comes crashing down on them. "Oh God, sorry! I meant— It's just—You're so sudden! Like, it all fell apart so quickly."

"Yeah," they numbly agree and push past the ache to explain. "Did you know most robots have perfect memories?" They start, then explain the entire Sentient Robots meeting.

When they're done, Lorena gapes at them for several seconds before frowning, opening her mouth to ask a question, then getting called away.

Purcell finishes their coffee while she works. When she returns, they expect a question, but she processes all over again.

After another long minute, Lorena rests her hand on Purcell's, holding the empty mug.

"I'm sorry they weren't what you were looking for."

Purcell used to be able to grit their teeth to prevent themselves from crying. Now, they can only lean away and hope she doesn't follow them.

Lorena leans forward and searches their face with such a tender expression that their lungs catch.

They duck down to hide their camera against their arm. Lorena squeezes their fingers while they calm down.

"Thank you," they whisper and sit up straight.

"Of course." She keeps searching for something.

"What?" they break and ask.

"Oh, um." She blinks rapidly, and her eyes go so wide that her upper eyelids disappear. "Uh…"

"You don't have to—"

"No, I'm trying to—"

"Just lie."

"'Lie'?" She giggles, and they relax now that her sad expression melts away. "I'm trying to… check my words before I speak this time."

They try to hide their shock, but she glances over them like she noticed anyway.

"You're… That was your lead-up?"

They nod.

"So what was the crash?"

They sigh, and luckily, she gets called away, so they plan out what to say. Tell her about the simulation and being human? Tallis and how he's both their killer and their closest aide? Her dismissal of their friendship and how it pushed them into reevaluating their reason for being here?

"Okay, sorry."

"You're okay," they mumble for the seventh or eighth time that she's apologized for working.

The two stare at each other while Purcell twitches uncomfortably and Lorena examines them.

"I uh… I don't remember exactly, but… I kind of… fidget when under stress."

Lorena frowns at their word choice but doesn't interrupt.

"And I guess I"—they lift their arms to show off the mangled wires—"picked at things for a while. Last night."

"'*Picked* at things'?" Lorena glowers and clutches at their twitchy, deconstructed forearm.

"I wasn't fully aware of it. I... I don't know. I wouldn't do it *now*."

"Yeah?" Lorena looks near tears, and it makes Purcell want to run back to their apartment. "That's good. Are you gonna be able to get it all fixed?"

Purcell watches their screen flash between yellow and pink in Lorena's glasses.

"I should, but... I don't want to."

She opens her mouth to argue, but they continue first.

"I feel bad for... destroying all his hard work. I don't want him to see me."

"I thought you didn't like your mechanic?"

"Eh..." They tip their head side to side. "He's okay. He's growing on me."

"That's nice?"

"It's a pain to get to him though, especially now that I'm... probably not waterproof anymore."

Lorena winces and pointedly stares at their shattered face.

"Do we need to wrap you up in something before sending you on your way?" She looks so genuine with her offer that Purcell balks and waves it off.

"No, no, no. I'd feel even worse if we... if he goes through all the trouble to fix me just for me to f—uh... mess it up again." They remember Corey at the last second, and Lorena's eyes soften as they edit their words.

The very next second, her jaw clenches, and Purcell feels under fire for something they probably deserve.

"Wha—" They start, but Lorena's called to help first. They're tempted to leave before learning the reason for that scary expression, but they wouldn't do that to her.

Some small shrapnel around their heart secretly hopes that she can convince them to go to Tallis. They feel warmed from more than the latte as they watch Lorena, and by extension Corey, flitting around the space.

The baby has wide, curious eyes that peer over her mom's shoulder constantly. She's completely silent, but they get the feeling she could be really loud if she wanted, judging by the healthy shine to her cheeks and the intelligent way she observes everyone.

Lorena returns with a smile like a grimace and hikes Corey up in the sling.

Corey giggles and drools in her mom's hair, and Purcell's non-existent heart melts.

"Such a mess," Lorena grumbles endearingly and pulls a handkerchief out of the sling's fold. She blindly pat dries her hair, back of her neck, and Corey's face.

Purcell's laughter at the scene quiets when she fixes them with a serious look.

"So, about your guilty conscience—"

They sputter, which genuinely sounds like they're dying because of their torn and obstructed valves.

"You need to take care of yourself, hon. You're not doing anyone a favor by feeling guilty for asking for help. We're gonna have to help you one way or another."

They sigh and flinch when Lorena grabs their hand.

Her tight grip makes them freeze, then flush pink with embarrassment when they see they were absentmindedly picking at the wires in their wrist. One is limp and pulled loose from wherever it's supposed to be connected inside their arm.

They let go of it and squeeze Lorena's fingers before awkwardly resting the offending hand in their lap.

"Will you go to him? Please?"

"Of course." It's easy to say to her pleading look. "I will, promise."

"Thank you." A wistful look crosses her face, and she zones out as Purcell uses the pause to lean over and look at Corey.

The baby squeals when she sees them, and it pulls Lorena back to the present.

"Where is your mechanic anyway? Is he far?"

"A little. Just across the southeast river."

Her eyes widen, but there's less shock than a warm light shines from her.

They make a lucky guess and ask, "Do you know Tallis?"

Lorena's face lights up in a blinding smile, and something acidic seeps over Purcell's thoughts.

"Oh, *Tallis*! He's so lovely! We went to school together! God, I haven't seen him in ages. How is he doing?" She leans close, and they hope their screen isn't disclosing the terrible corrosion they feel in their gut.

Just once, they want to make a connection here that doesn't tie them back to their old life. They want to meet someone completely separated from the persistent grief that comes with Tallis and their strange rebirth.

They want to run away and move somewhere no one will remind them of pianos or loss or sentience filings or mechanics ever again.

"Purcell?"

They blink rapidly as Lorena's face comes back into focus, despite every blink functionally doing nothing—their vision never ends.

"Sorry. Thinking." They're scared by how stricken she looks, like they had done more than zone out for a moment.

"Oh, God, I was worried you had like, blue-screened or something."

They snort at the thought.

"Blue?"

"Yeah. You went all blue." She gestures at their screen. "Your face stayed though, so…" She tries to shrug, but winces at the added weight around her.

"Interesting." They shake themselves and commit to remembering to ask about their screen colors later. "But anyway, yeah. He's good. He's in a… place by the river and has a bunch of robots wheelin' around helping out. 'S like a metal zoo in there," they joke until Lorena smiles.

"And he… What did he say…?" They mumble and look off to the side. "He saw me in a collection center recently, bought me, patched me up, and uh…" They pause at Lorena's shocked look, but she waits for them to finish. "He woke me up. I moved into the city… Met you."

She properly gasps this time. "That's so recent!"

"Yeah."

"No wonder you didn't know anyone! God, sorry. If I'd known, I wouldn't've—"

"Please, you're fine." They reach out to reassure her, and she clutches their hand with both of hers.

"Goodness, honey. And speaking of which, when are you gonna bring me those papers to fill out for you?"

"Uh…"

Truthfully, they had expected her to go back and say she wouldn't do it after seemingly trying to let them down easy last time.

"I'll have to print them first. And I'll have a bunch of sh—Uh.

Things to do first before that step. Like, background checks and stuff."

"Alright. You just let me know, okay?"

"Okay." Purcell stays until the line grows for the after-work rush.

The sun will be going down soon, and they don't want to get caught out at night again. They say goodbye to Lorena and Corey before walking to their apartment.

Now that their appearance is even worse, most people move around them like they're diseased. People stare but won't make eye contact.

They sigh as they reach their room finally, eyeing the paper tag '5370' posted beside their front door. They keep forgetting they can change it now.

The door whines as it shuts, and they turn to hold the knob and throw themselves into the door to latch it. They hear it click along with a terrible crunching noise as the loose plastic in their shoulder sinks into the foam under their skin.

Chapter 14

The library printer can only be used if you have a library card, and you can only get a library card as a robot if you have proof of sentience.

"For fucks' sake," Purcell mutters as they stop filling out the form.

They grumble and cover their face with their hands as they try to form a plan B.

"Y'alright? Aren't you—Oh, you are! Hi!" A woman greets them, and it takes a second for Purcell to remember.

"Crystal?"

"Yeah!" she cheers and fills the space at the counter beside them easily. She still wobbles a little, and they glance down to see that her metal leg is that same flowery one that's too tall.

"How've you been?" Crystal asks and leans close to read the form they were working through.

They answer by sighing and waving over the damned sentience-number space that they left blank.

They explain their dilemma to her, and she mutters the entire time as she prints for them herself. "Damned rules … unnecessary … Don't know why they … too many dumb roadblocks … Here you go, honey." She hands them three copies.

"Oh, I only needed—Well, thank you."

"'S no problem, dear. I gave you one extra in case someone messes up. Gotta write in pen 'nd all."

"Ah, okay. Thank you."

"Anytime!" She pats their shoulder like a sports coach, leaning around to see the front desk. "You should try and get a card anyway. Tell 'em you're in the process of filing, and they might just give you one." She winks.

"You think so? I guess it doesn't hurt to ask."

"Yeah! Worst thing they can say is 'No.'" She pats their shoulder again, and this time they notice the concerned once-over she gives them.

They wince and wait for her to ask, but she doesn't.

"Alright, well, I gotta get to work, but you take care of yourself, alright?"

"I will. Thank you again."

She sweetly smiles and nods. "It's no trouble. If it happens again, just ask around. I'm sure there'll always be someone willing to help."

"I will."

"Good. Now, I've got a bunch of kiddos to read to. Good luck!"

"You too!" Purcell waves as she heads to the kids' section—decorated like a forest and full of parents milling around with their children.

They grab a free folder from the stationery section by the front desk, then hover for an anxious moment before approaching an employee. They feel better being able to clutch something to their chest, despite the logical part of their brain acknowledging that a manila folder of legal documents isn't going to save them.

They find the courage to approach the desk while wondering if they have a brain.

"Hi? Um... I have a question?"

The man behind the desk looks up from his computer and waits.

"Okay. I'm in the middle of filing for sentience, and I know your paperwork says I can't file for uh... a library card without—"

"No, you'll have to wait."

"Oh. Okay, sorry. I was just wondering."

"Yeah, that's fine, but if the judge decides 'No', then we can't have you walkin' around with a card and no personhood."

"Ah... That makes sense, okay."

He turns back to the computer, and even though he didn't speak unkindly, the clinical way he spoke pings through them like a hot iron.

With no plan, Purcell turns and runs into the bathroom.

They lock themselves in a stall and press their forehead to the door, hugging the folder tight. A sob erupts from them, and they stifle the noise when someone else enters.

They know they're unsuccessful when the stranger pauses. "Sweetie, are you alright?"

"Y-yeah." Purcell shrinks down in embarrassment at their broken voice.

"What happened? You can tell me—Good to get it off your chest."

They clutch the papers before releasing a breath and looking down at the folder.

"I'm um..." They decide not to disclose being a robot, unsure that the woman will continue to be empathetic if she knows. "Dealing with a legal thing, and it's taking a long time—or, it's a lot of hoops and… and roadblocks. And I'm not even sure I want it or if it's *worth* it, so—" Purcell breaks off into sobs, and the woman murmurs reassurances through the wall.

"You'll make it through, sweetie. You sound strong."

"Th-thank you." They try to pull themselves together, but it's harder with the kind words from the other stall.

"Make sure to take care of yourself, alright? Spend some time outside. Talk to people. You'll be okay," she whispers like she's clutching their hands in hers.

"I'll try," they promise.

"I believe in you, honey. For what it's worth, a random stranger believes in you." She chuckles to herself as she washes her hands.

"Thank you," they repeat, then sigh as the door creaks open and closed.

They count to 30, then leave the library.

For their own sake, they choose to believe that she still would have been kind if she could have seen them.

Chapter 15

It's a dry, dark night when Purcell gains the courage to go to Tallis.

They remember the creaking of their body as they became shakier over the course of the two hours. They remember stumbling in the gravel and falling flat on their face partway through the treacherous journey. They remember their relief seeing the garage door open at the end. They don't remember entering.

And they certainly don't remember why they would be stretched out on the kitchen floor of all things.

Purcell groans and tries to sit up. A sharp inhale to their right makes them jump.

"Oh, God." They clutch at their heart, then flinch when Tallis reaches for them.

"Easy. Don't push yourself." He helps them into a seated position.

"Ugh. Hey." They wince and look over their body. "I'm sorry."

"No, no. Don't worry." He looks concerned, and it makes them feel worse. "How are you feeling?"

"Physically?"

He frowns more.

"Sorry. I'm uh… a lot better," they admit and savor being able to move without their joints grinding.

"Okay, good." He tentatively reaches to lay a hand on their shoulder.

Purcell leans with the weight of it. Their chin taps the top of his hand before they gain the courage to look at his face.

He looks relieved, and it hits them then how badly they must have been hurt.

"I'm sorry," they say again. They don't think they'll be able to say it enough.

"Stop, stop, just—" He cuts off and sighs, but it seems directed at himself. "I'm glad you came."

They nod—a silent promise.

"Will you stay for dinner?" he asks, and the smile on their face surprises them too.

"Sure," they whisper.

Dinner is an awkward affair as Tallis cooks a gorgeous pasta dish that Purcell would feel guilty for eating.

"When I can taste, I'll take you up on it," they argue again. "For now, just looking is enough. I don't want to… remove any from you for no reason."

Tallis sighs but eventually acquiesces.

He hasn't asked them what happened, which they're grateful for. They share small talk about random happenings and potential upgrades before he carefully turns the conversation.

"You've been here two days, by the way."

"Oh." They'd assumed it was just one.

"Yeah… Random restarts are a bad sign, so…"

"Restart? How did you know I…" Purcell cuts themselves off. He means last night, not the other day in the bathroom.

"Did it happen before?" He wipes his lips with a napkin and examines them with pinched eyebrows.

"Um… just once before. And… I was beeping the other day, but it stopped quickly after I noticed it."

"Hm… Were you overheating?"

Purcell sits back to think.

He clears the table, saving the leftovers that could have been Purcell's.

"No, I was… nervous though."

"Sometimes panic will force a restart. You were probably beeping to warn you."

They hum and nod.

He asks them a few more technical questions as he washes

dishes. They get caught up on the clanging when he acciden-tally drops a fork. It slid out from his soapy fingers, but he caught it after it smacked the metal basin.

The visual reminds them of all the things they've bumped against, dropped, knocked over, since waking up in this garage a few weeks ago.

Tallis barely blinks at the slip-up, so used to the clumsiness that they never used to experience.

They ask before putting their thoughts together. "Would simulations have perfect—like, smoothened-out experience, or life, I mean? I didn't used to drop things or… break things… lose things…" They grow quiet when he turns.

They're sitting at a pseudo-workbench dining table, newly patched together, and broiling in guilt.

"Short answer… yes."

"And the long one?"

He sits down at their side of the table and takes a deep breath. "Long answer is… it could be a variety of things. You've probably changed significantly from… a month ago. Part of it could be… not a sim, and part of it could be… stress."

They sigh. "That makes sense."

"You're blue," he says like they're supposed to know what that means.

"Yeah?" They sit up straighter, trying to seem more put together.

"Thank you for coming to me."

Purcell slowly nods. "Could you… Is there a quick way for me to… Uh."

"You can ask, you know. Nothing is too weird."

They flush at the many ideas that gives them. "Well… when you put it like *that*," they joke to release the tense air.

Tallis's eyes widen like they've performed an opera for him.

"I want to blink. I want to be able to blink."

"Oh." He immediately stands, but when he opens a drawer, he hesitates. "Did you…" He turns around to show his palms. "This isn't bad—an accusation. I need to know so I don't make it worse."

They balk at the preface, and he continues.

"Was some of your damage from you peeling at stuff?"

Purcell exhales hard and goes very still. "I… Not on purpose."

He frowns and waits for them to explain.

"I… blacked out. Woke up to being peeled like a clove of garlic."

He laughs but quickly stifles it. "Okay. So if I put something that sticks out on you, are you going to peel it off?"

They want to say *No*, but their pause speaks for them.

"Okay. The other way will require some coding. That's why I—"

"'Coding'!?"

He shows his palms again, and they hate the thought of someone rooting around in their brain—their memories, their thoughts.

Purcell starts to leave, and Tallis panics behind them.

"We don't have to! There's surely another option. I'll just have to look for—"

"What's the first option?" They stop to ask, even though everything within them wants to run.

"It's like a sticker that covers your eyes when you want to blink."

They relax a little, less poised to escape.

"But it's kinda bumpy. You'll be able to feel it on your face."

"Is there a version that's okay to take on and off?"

"Um… yeah, actually. I'll just teach you how to place it and… that should work." He turns to rummage through a workbench, doesn't find it, then goes through a bin of plastic parts.

The doghouse-looking robot home activates when he gets close, and the one-wheeled bot beeps like it's waking up. It rolls its wheel a few times, then zips excitedly around his feet.

"Why do you… Are they like pets?" Purcell points at the robot.

It stops to face them when they reference it. They hadn't realized it could hear or understand them.

"It doesn't do anything, does it?"

"No, just cute," he answers simply before turning to brandish a pill-shaped sticker. "This way, your display eyes won't always close when your actual eyes close, but…" He shrugs, and they sit down to receive it.

"So this bar goes right between the lenses." He gives them a quick lesson on how to position the sticker, then does it for them.

There's a strange pull, like a magnet, between their eyes before something beeps. The tension releases, and they blink.

Purcell gasps, then intentionally blinks again. They catch Tallis's pleased smile before closing their eyes for several seconds and relaxing into nothingness.

Purcell sighs and sinks into their chair as they finally feel like they're resting after days of being *on*.

"You don't sleep, right?" Tallis asks a millisecond before they mention it.

Purcell smiles and answers with their eyes still closed. "No. I've tried, but nothing happens."

"Do you want to?"

They open their eyes. "It would be nice," they admit.

"Okay. I'll look into finding the right cord for you."

"Okay." They nod, then close their eyes. "This is *so* satisfying."

They falter at the awkward air.

Tallis is fidgeting with other parts and tools—very pointedly not looking at them, but a closer look reveals that he's inspecting invisible dust and not doing anything.

"Do you want me out of your hair?" They tense up, ready to stand.

"*No*, no." He stills after his quick reaction.

"Thank you."

They both tense after their awkward statement. They *meant* it despite sounding uncomfortable, and they hope he can tell.

"Um… Do you want to… Well." He cuts off and looks to the side.

Purcell blinks, waiting.

"I was going to say you could sleep here, but…"

"Oh." They turn to the dark sky outside.

He closed the garage door during dinner, but there are several windows scattered around the shed.

"Yeah, I can stay. I'd hate to get jumped again and ruin all your—"

Tallis gasps like he's been hit.

Purcell realizes their mistake. "Oh! I—I didn't—"

Tallis lurches forward like he'll hug them, but he's so tense they don't think he could lift his arms if he tried.

For the first time, they watch as a dark flicker of anger passes behind his eyes.

As quickly as it appeared, it's smothered. His gaze wanders over them, mapping out the old damage from that awful night.

"As loath as I am to tell you what to do…" He starts, and the steel undercurrent in his gentle, mossy voice makes Purcell listen closely. "Clothes would help you a lot with… people like that."

They both hold still, watching the other observe the person in front of them like they're brand new.

"You'll probably have to go to specialty shops for it." Tallis mentally surveys them like a stylist. He points at their nonexistent waist—just pistons that act as a spine. "Pants in particular are hard to find… And you don't seem like the dress type."

"Ah… not really. Except for special occasions."

"Yeah?" He turns to yawn.

They ignore the conversational olive branch and stand up. "Come on. I may not need to sleep, but *you* do."

He laughs as they usher him back to the bedroom side of the shed.

"What are you going to do? I should at least try to keep you company."

His one-wheeled robot pet beeps and whirs excitedly beside him. They wonder if he ever cuddles with it like a dog.

"No. Don't worry about it." They wave away his concern. "I've gotten used to… waiting out the night."

"You can watch something?" He points to the chair facing the blank wall they'd joked about last time.

"Okay."

He shows them how to work the screenless TV before getting ready for bed.

"Have fun! Good night!"

"You too!"

"And don't vanish in the morning. I'd like to see you."

They falter at his honesty. He's crawled up the ladder to the lofted bed already, so they blankly stare at the paused intro to a random movie.

"I won't."

"Okay, good."

And true to their word, they watch movies with the volume real low and subtitles on until the sun comes up.

They finish three movies before stopping early and wandering around the garage now that there's daylight. The little, wheeled bot put itself to bed at some point during the night, and Purcell skims the papers strewn around to get a better feel for what Tallis does all day.

One table is dedicated to PRL models—research essays, online reviews, advertisements, and (the most damning) an article on simulation side effects. This must be the Purcell table.

They've been intentionally not touching anything, only looking at what's out in the open, but they pick up the simulation article to read thoroughly. It takes them a minute to realize this is a critique of the paper they read a month ago. This author picks apart the previous one for several errors and red flags, including the word choices that have 'robot-exclusionary language'.

They read with a dull sense of satisfaction as this article tears into the older one for saying 'damage to the human mind' instead of recognizing all sentient minds, and for depicting dysphoria as related to anger disorders as opposed to its own, distinct symptom of long-term simulations. This article is much kinder to the people entering the real world than the first one Purcell read.

They jump when an alarm sounds, throwing the packet on the table like they've been caught stealing.

Tallis shifts in bed. Then the alarm cuts off.

Purcell returns to the armchair below him to wait. His alarm goes off nine minutes later, and he silences it immediately the second time.

The wooden loft creaks as he makes his way down the ladder.

"Hey," he mutters lowly like he's still half asleep and doesn't wait for them to reply before turning to the kitchen.

Purcell watches him make tea and begin rifling through the fridge.

They move to a rolling chair behind him and watch him make a cheese omelet.

"Want one?" He glances over his shoulder, but doesn't have the energy to make it all the way to actually look at them.

"No, no. Don't worry."

"'Kay."

They spend a quiet morning together.

"What did you end up watching?" he asks as he does the dishes.

"Some old horror movies."

"Yeah? Any good?"

They smile at his low-energy questions. They like knowing he isn't a morning person.

They also learn that he's a horror fan too, and they rave about an old vampire movie before Purcell decides to head out.

"This was... nice," they whisper in the calm air.

"Good. I'm glad you... I enjoyed it too." He buffers for a second like he'll say something wrong, but then moves on. "Text me and come back any time—Not that you'd need to text before, but separately, I mean. Do both."

Purcell gestures for him to relax. "Will do."

"Good." His tense shoulders fall.

They wave goodbye and savor the quiet walk home. All

their joints move silently again, so it's a calming riverside stroll before navigating the city streets.

They reach their apartment door and turn back around to visit the office downstairs.

There's a woman behind the desk on the phone, but she purses her lips toward an empty chair for Purcell to wait in and be spoken to next.

A minute later, she hangs up and says, "What can I do for you?"

They sit up straighter and hope she thinks they're a person.

"How can I change my name on my door? Like, myself? Or, it changed legally and—"

"Oh. Maintenance does it." She turns and starts typing on the computer. Her acrylic nails click louder than the keys. "Which room?"

They tell her.

"Okay. I put your request in. Someone should be by later today."

"Cool. Thank you." They stand to leave.

"Will that be all?" She smiles up at them.

"Yes. Thank you."

"You're welcome."

Two hours later, there's a knock at their door.

"Maintenance!" is called, muffled.

Purcell opens the door to a man who could pass as Tallis's brother.

"Hi."

"Hi," he copies and points at the tag on the door. "Changin' this?"

"Yes, please."

"T' what?"

"Purcell…" They spell it for him and watch as he replaces the little slip of paper. He puts the '5370' one in his pocket.

"You change it legally?"

"Yeah… Yes." They don't know how casual to be with him. It doesn't look like he'll really care.

"'S good. You doin' sentience next?"

They blink, surprised he knows.

"… Yes."

"Yeah. You're in our system as a robot, so—" He shrugs and puts his hands in his pockets.

"Oh." They nod. "Yeah. It's next. Just got the paperwork printed for it."

He examines their face closely. "Filing in Mecklenburg County?"

"Yes."

"Recommend you go early on Mondays. Talk to Sandra."

"Okay?"

"She worked with me… a while ago. Got my papers with her help. 'S a real sweet girl—knows Spanish."

"Ah." Purcell relaxes now that they're not in that unsolicited advice limbo. He's actually helping. "Thank you."

"'Course. I hope it goes well."

"Thanks! Me too."

He smiles politely and steps back. "A'right. You take care, Purcell."

"You too!" They take their time closing the door as he walks away.

Chapter 16

Purcell finds Sandra's email on the County Clerk website. She's registered as part of Immigration Staff, but she replies to Purcell's questions with all the PDFs and predicted costs that the website was vague about.

They reply to her with a 'Thank you so much!!' and double-check the affidavit forms that Crystal printed are up to date before going to find Lorena.

Purcell orders their typical, free latte and sits at the counter.

Lorena sets their mug in front of them but takes several minutes to work through the post-work rush before she can say hello.

They sip carefully to preserve their foam bunny as long as possible.

The manila folder of paperwork is perched beside them, and they reflexively open it to check that the papers haven't spontaneously disappeared several times.

"Purcell!" Lorena cheers when she finally has a free moment.

"Lorena!" They copy and drum their fingers on the folder.

"Is that what I think it is?"

"Yep!" They push it toward her, and she excitedly snatches it up to read. "Nice! I can do this today, if you want."

"It's no hurry. I haven't even asked my second person yet."

"You need two?" She looks up through her eyelashes.

"Mhm." They tentatively nod.

"That's a lot."

"I *know*." They jokingly wave forward, pointing out their status as a regular at the café—how desperate they are to ask their barista.

"Well, you did just move here." Lorena defends them like they're being serious.

"'Moved' is putting it nicely."

She winces but laughs when they laugh.

Purcell spends several hours chatting on and off with her, even introducing themselves to her coworker finally, until closing.

Lorena lets them stay until the two are shutting off the lights and locking the door behind them.

"Thank you for letting me loiter a bit," they joke and take a polite step back to leave.

"Oh! Do you have to go?" Lorena loosely reaches for them.

"Well… no."

"Um. My mom will have Corey for a little while longer if you wanna hang out outside of work for once." She waves up at the purple and yellow brick building.

"Sounds good!" They step back up to slightly loom over her.

They're kind of tall, but Lorena is also really short, so they feel like a giant beside her.

She squints a bright smile at them before threading their arms together and leading them toward the shopping district side of the street.

"Did you have something in mind?" they ask.

"Honestly… no." She chuckles nervously, but Purcell didn't expect her to have plans. "I'm mostly just excited to be able to walk around without a stroller and all her stuff."

"Ah…" They nod. "That's good then…"

She glances at them curiously.

"Because you're leading us to the most crowded part of town."

She smiles and jokingly pushes them away, but keeps their arms linked.

The two pass several clothing stores before Purcell gains the courage to mention their look-more-sentient plan.

"Would you…"

Lorena looks up with cute, doe eyes.

"Be willing to clothes shop with me?"

She gasps before accepting the mission.

They go in and out of a few stores, trying to find things that work on their thin, frame-only body they're sporting. Eventually, they give up on human stores, and Lorena finds a robot's clothing store within walking distance.

Purcell stills when they walk through the door. The Sleeping Beauty robot works here.

She spots them right away, and her human, silicone face expresses her shock clearly.

"Hi." No point in ignoring the fact that they know each other.

"*Hi.*" She glances between them and Lorena, buffering. "How are you? How's the… process?"

"It's good… Did you call Tallis?"

"I *did*…" She stares ahead like she's debating adding more detail.

Lorena awkwardly coughs before weaseling away to look at clothes.

"He… pointed me in the direction of a local fix, so… thank you."

"Yeah? I'm glad it was helpful."

"Yeah."

They use the lull to locate Lorena and escape the conversation.

"Let me know if you need any help!"

"We will!" Purcell gives a thumbs-up before ducking behind a rack to hide their face against Lorena's shoulder. She quietly giggles but doesn't mention it until they're out of the small shop.

The human clothing stores had Condition 3 options for a limited number of things that Purcell could get, but this robot one does not, so Lorena buys pants for them with an I-owe-you deal.

"Thank you again."

She smiles and shakes her head after they repeat themselves a third time. They can't help but keep thanking her because, despite her reassurances, there's a strange stiffness in how she's walking around. It's like she's conflicted about being out with them—happy they're finding clothes but looking like she wants to be doing something else. Maybe it's because Corey is elsewhere. Purcell doesn't know what else it could be.

"Here. Do you want to put something on now?" She opens up the bag for them to peer into.

"Um... Yeah, actually." Purcell digs out the pair of pants she just bought and a sweater from earlier. It looks similar to an old sweater of theirs from the simulation, and they feel a bittersweet twinge in their gut every time they look at it.

They step into the mouth of an alleyway, and Lorena watches as they slip into clothes for the first time in a month.

"Feel good?"

"Yeah!" They grin and lift their arms like they're presenting something. "Do I look like a person?"

"*Eh...*" Lorena teases, then laughs when they gasp, fake-offended. "You look more... people-y. Yes."

"'People-y'? Is that the technical term?" They step out and reach to take the bag.

Lorena scoffs and crosses her arms. "Yes, it is! As of—Oh." She notices and hands over the bag. "Here."

"Thanks."

"It's no problem, hon. I'm glad I could help."

"You were a great help," they say genuinely, getting close to speak softer.

Lorena smiles, then falters and reaches for the bag.

"Hm?" They stick their arm out and watch her pull the folder out. "Oh, yes. That's important."

She tucks it securely against her chest. "I know you said it was no rush, but are you sure you don't want me to do it now?"

"I mean... If you want to, I certainly won't stop you."

"Okay. Let's sit, then." She leads them to a bench and rereads the instructions on the form.

As she's writing, Purcell keeps their eyes on the city to avoid looking over her shoulder.

Lorena writes about their character and as close to real proof as she can get that they're sentient. When she's done, she offers it to read, but they decline.

"So who was that terribly stiff robot back at Carmine's Closet?"

They sigh heavily, and Lorena giggles. She pulls out her phone to search something, so they have an easier time being honest.

"Remember the robot support group?"

She glances up curiously before looking back down at her phone.

As Purcell retells the Sleeping Beauty story, Lorena guides them to some undisclosed location.

"Where are you taking us?" they ask after she huffs again at how they were treated by their so-called peers.

"My bank."

"Oh." Purcell follows her in and is then pleasantly surprised when a staff member greets them with a real smile. The entire notary process goes smoothly, and every employee talks to Purcell like they're really thinking and listening.

The two leave barely five minutes later, and Lorena passes the completed paperwork over for Purcell to keep.

"Thank you again."

"Of course! I know me. If we hadn't done it today, I never would've finished it," she admits, then freezes with wide eyes. She turns, flailing to explain, but they're simply amused. "Not that this isn't important! I've just got a terrible habit of setting things down and forgetting—Doing it all at once is really helpful for me, so I don't lose the momentum of—"

Purcell gently rests a hand on her arm, and she pauses to breathe. She moves on when it's clear they aren't judging.

The two window-shop downtown for another hour, with Lorena occasionally checking her phone when her mom sends her updates on Coriander. She seems lighter now, and they're glad the reluctance from earlier is dissipating.

Purcell tenses up when it gets dark, but they try to hide it. It's easier to feel safe with Lorena by their side anyway. Between the company and the clothes, they're feeling much more comfortable in crowds.

When Lorena's feet start hurting, they find a bench by the river to wind down.

"Can I ask you a personal question?" Lorena prefaces,

breaking the amicable silence.

"Sure," they say lightly.

"You're 29."

"Yeah."

"But you said Tallis turned you on recently?"

Purcell blinks at the unfortunate wording. The wall in front of them lights up pink as their screen gives them away, and Lorena gasps.

"I mean—Sorry!"

The two laugh together so hard that extra fans turn on inside Purcell's chest.

Lorena recovers her breath, leaning against their side. "You know, when you whirr this loud, it sounds like you're purring."

Their orange screen morphs back into a pink, and the wall in front of them resembles a creamsicle during the switch.

"Yeah?"

"Mhm." She hums sleepily, but then sits up.

Purcell misses the weight of her on their frame.

"But you know what I meant. Your age. How are you…"

"29 when I've been dead for a while?"

Lorena gives them a concerned look when they accidentally reveal the answer.

So Purcell explains.

They tell her about their last birthday and their last concert. They tell her about the storm, Tallis's chair, and undoing the restraints. The group of kids and the elephant folder. Blacking out. The pasta dinner. Their piano.

She takes it all in, nodding and asking close questions.

"What are some of the differences? Like, the clumsiness you said."

The two talk about dewy grass and static.

Lorena smiles at their assumption that they would zap people with the electricity.

"You know that does happen? Between humans too."

"Really? Does it hurt?"

"Only a little. It's more *shocking* than anything." She digs her elbow into them, but they missed her joke.

"What?"

"Ugh. I'm *hilarious*. You don't—"

"Sorry," Purcell laughs. They eventually convince her that they truly didn't understand, so she explains static shocks to them.

When her phone buzzes again, it's to ask her to get Corey.

Lorena sighs and reluctantly stands to leave.

"Walk with you?" Purcell offers.

"Please."

They walk a few more blocks side-by-side.

"Don't worry about coming in," Lorena says, barring them from entering the privacy gate in front of a townhome. "I'll be in and out. Otherwise, we'll be here forever. My mom's a talker."

"Okay." Purcell laughs, silently relieved that there was a good reason for them not to enter the house.

True to her word, Lorena exits with a stroller a few minutes later.

"Still stickin' around?" she jokes like the baby could convince them to leave.

"If you'll let me."

"Of course."

They have a very short walk to Lorena's apartment building, and she yawns as she wishes Purcell a good night.

"You too!" They smile, hiding the dread of going back to

their empty apartment alone.

There's a strange lull as Purcell thinks about their poor decorating and Lorena stares up at them. She looks concerned by whatever their screen is doing, so they try to think happier thoughts.

"Hug good night?" she asks, reaching out to pull them back into the present moment.

"Sure!" They lean down to hug her and whisper another thank you for the pants and affidavit.

Lorena is tense and awkwardly pats their back. They take the hint and step away.

She fidgets with the stroller's handle and keeps looking at them like a deer in headlights.

"Are you alright?" They tamp down the instinct to reach out to reassure her.

"Yes!" She squeaks and nods a suspiciously long time.

"Okay... I'll see you soon?"

"Yes," she breathes out as her tense shoulders fall. "Actually, I meant to—Well, I don't want to tell you what to—Not that I think—"

"Lena."

"Sorry." She reaches to pat their arm, but doesn't make it all the way before she curls in to brush the choppy back of her hair. "I know that one support group fell through, but I think... I want to very lightly.... suggest... trying another one."

Purcell nods.

"Peers are... good. I don't want you to feel alone. I think you can find a similar, uh... mentality. Eventually... I hope."

"Well, I hope so too." Purcell jokes and feels warmth bloom in their chest when she laughs.

Lorena swats them jokingly and looks to say something else,

but falters when Corey wakes up and starts cooing.

"Oh. We're gonna go, but—"

"No worries!" They step away as her frantic energy ramps up.

"Good night!" she says again and waves.

They smile and wave back before walking home, with the bag bumping their leg the whole way.

Chapter 17

"So, what do you do for fun?" the other bot asks them, drumming her fingers on the lip of her pint glass.

"Uh… I walk a lot." Purcell winces after the weak sentence, but Eva's screen face doesn't give away any sign of judgment. "Across Providence Road, usually. I walk there almost every day."

"Into Highway 16?"

"Yeah."

She takes a sip of her drink and nods. Her head has two parts, so she has a lower jaw that moves when she talks and drinks, but her eyes are on a screen.

"That does sound nice. I'm more of a homebody. This is the main thing that gets me out of the house." She gestures to their table, where the rest of the robots are chatting.

Purcell found an ad for their group that meets every Saturday at Last World Brewery and decided to take Lorena's advice. It was labeled as a Robots' Social Hour and didn't have the word 'sentient' anywhere in the description, but they assumed it was right regardless. And it is.

They're comfortable enough in this group to drink their water and make small talk this time. The bots here are strange. In a relaxing, authentic way.

The employees also recognized who Purcell was looking for and politely pointed them in the right direction. Overall, they're finding it easy to let their guard down.

A super tiny bot hops off their stool to join Purcell and Eva.

"Are you new? I've never seen you before."

"Ah, I am." They try not to stare.

This little robot has two long arms that worked like hooks to lift them onto the stool. They have one large, grippy tire and a wide, screen face. On the ground, they were barely two feet tall. Purcell can't imagine how many people probably think they're a delivery bot and nothing more.

"And before you ask—Yes. I do like this body, and I will be keeping it."

Purcell flushes bright pink when they realize they froze anyway.

"Sorry! I was just hoping that you don't get kicked around as much as I have."

Eva gasps and goes to reassure one of them. Her outstretched hand between them flops on the table, ignored, as the little bot bursts out laughing.

"Well, a pleasure to meet you—"

"Purcell."

"Purcell! I'm True. And believe it or not, people tend to leave me alone..." They fade out, and their pixels flicker like a twitchy eye. "Or take pictures, but that, I can ignore."

"Oh, well... I want to say that's good, but..."

True shrugs their thin arms. "Ya get far enough away from a human and they think you're cute. You get too close, and they get creeped out. Just depends on which you wanna be. Or, you get the lucky draw and look human enough that they treat you normal." They snort and change the subject. "You and Eva gettin' along? She start talkin' about her board game yet?"

"'Board game'?"

Eva grins and starts rambling.

Purcell tries to pay attention, but after the third aside about different types of migration patterns in waterfowl, they start wishing they could get drunk. They don't think that's a thing Tallis can do for them, but they commit to asking later.

A pitchy, obnoxious coo from the other end of the table pulls everyone's attention.

"Well, aren't y'all just the cutest!?" A middle-aged woman reaches to pat one of the bots at the end like they're a dog.

She's too drunk to notice how they tense up but decide to just let her touch them unprompted.

"What," comes out of Purcell's mouth by reflex. They're about to tell her off when Eva catches their eye and subtly shakes her head.

They stay quiet as the woman goes on about how her sister-in-law has a live-in robot that's getting a degree in creative writing and how isn't that just amazing that y'all can channel all your hardship into something so artistic and wow, it's so inspiring how so many of you are able to act like real people now!

"Isn't it lovely! I've always been supportive of robot rights! I hope all of you are successful and find love, and oh! I just love how well y'all blend in with the rest of us nowadays! It's so cute seeing you do real jobs and drink and marry each other like real people!"

"What the fuck?" Purcell quietly hisses to Eva, and she shrugs with her eyes wide and palms showing.

Finally, the lady leaves, but Purcell barely waits for her to be out of earshot before asking again, "What the hell was that!?"

True laughs awkwardly and drums their arms on the table before asking, "That's never happened to you before?"

"*No?* Does she think we're all children!?"

"Probably," another bot further down answers. He said hello early on, and he has an interesting grill around his human-like face that gives the look of a beard.

He takes a very human-like sip of his beer before turning back to the others.

Purcell sighs and closes their eyes to rub the seams of their face.

Eva giggles at their dramatics and attempts to guide the conversation to lighter things. They can't commit to talking about language-learning over the weird, offensive woman who had talked at them.

They replay it over and over in their mind, imagining all the ways they could have insulted her to make her reconsider the infantilized view of them.

A crunchy, static sound erupts from their torso, and a few bots give them uncomfortable glances as they sit there rumbling like an engine, mulling it over.

"You good?" True asks.

"Ugh. Yes." They keep murmuring expletives until they calm themselves down.

True chuckles good-naturedly and pushes Purcell's water closer like it will help.

"Thanks." They play along with the joke and take a long sip while Eva keeps questioning the most ethical way to learn Cantonese.

She could download the language straight, but would never have the emotional connection to individual words and phrases that she could have by learning slower in a community, piece by piece. True is arguing for downloading the language files and then joining a language-learning club anyway. Then, Eva could practice the accuracies in real life, apart from the technically correct, stiff version.

Purcell nods along. Looking at all the robots at the table gives them ideas for future upgrades. They especially like Eva's face. She doesn't have any silicone, but the movement of her jaw is nice.

They also like the idea of having a screen that doesn't display their emotions like the one they have now.

The bot that the bearded one is listening to has two antenna-like nubs on her head that look like cat ears, which Purcell really likes as a middle ground between not feeling bald and not wanting hair.

A few robots leave right at an hour, but Eva and two others stay.

The one that endured being pet by that woman seems actually tipsy, and Purcell is trying to find a way to ask if this is their personality or if they're intoxicated. They wonder if the bot is drinking more because of that horrid interaction earlier, and the tension in their chest spikes again.

They've spent most of the time listening, so they don't feel familiar enough to ask personal questions. The self-imposed isolation makes them even more annoyed.

"I'm gonna head out," Purcell says and stands.

Eva gives a cute smile and waves, not wanting to interrupt the other.

Purcell tips back the last of their water at the same time the one speaking lifts their glass in a silent farewell.

They nod back before leaving. A nervous energy thrums through them. Their fingers twitch as they imagine getting the anger out by playing some Beethoven.

Instead, they walk to Tallis's to mention upgrade ideas. They're farther than normal, and the sun is already low, but they have clothes on. They don't want to be scared of the dark forever. Hopefully nothing happens.

The walk is so long from Last World that they actually get bored and look into the river a few times.

The water looks sluggish and dark. It's far, far below the tallest waterline on the retaining wall, so they assume it's due for some rain.

"Shit!" Purcell stops in their tracks and turns around.

It's too late now. They should have grabbed the affidavit form.

"Damn it," they mutter and turn again to keep walking. They'll just have to remember next time.

They reach the dirt road, walk around the garage, and find the door open.

They step up to knock on the wall as they enter. Only to stop right in their tracks.

Their arm is still raised to knock.

Tallis isn't alone, and he and his guest *definitely* don't know that Purcell is here.

They move to silently back away, but a part of them is really enjoying the unexpected show.

Not that they can see much. Really, they're just looking at Tallis's broad back where he's pinning someone against the kitchen counter as they make out.

A small, pale hand reaches around his waist to scratch at his shoulder blades.

A quiet groan and a shift closer from Tallis sends Purcell back into their body, and they shake themselves to stop staring.

They continue the silent backpedal.

When Tallis tilts his head, they finally see the other person.

Purcell's whole body goes rigid. Then, they turn on their heel and walk away, not thinking about being quiet anymore. Not when Tallis is busy with *Lorena*.

They kick at the gravel more than they should as they stomp back up the road.

Of course. The first friend they make in the real world has to be interested in the fucker that murdered them.

They thought they'd mostly forgiven Tallis for waking them, but seeing him wrapped up with Lorena reignited all of that betrayal, hearing "You're alright" and "It's okay" that first night.

They wonder what he said to Lorena to have her hips pressed back against that dusty countertop.

Purcell makes that clicky, growling noise as they climb the stairs to the bridge in record time.

It's dark, with the sun only a sliver of red bleeding across the river on the west side.

Purcell crosses the almost-empty highway and finds a significant break in the concrete to sit and watch the sunset. Their legs swing freely over the water below.

They're tired of walking. Tired of thinking.

Tired of trying to fit in here and tired of this damned, never-ending, music-less world.

Their twitchy hand pulls them out of their thoughts, and they look down to see the wires plucked out and limp.

Purcell sighs and slumps forward to rest their face in their hands.

The affected palm burns under the pressure, but they ignore it. If they're going to keep breaking their hand, the least they can do is suffer the consequences.

They brush over the bump of the sticker on their lenses, but the knowledge that they could peel it off just to restick it prevents them from messing with it.

They want to break something that can't be fixed.

"Purcell?" a familiar, sweet voice calls off to their left.

They lift their head to see Lorena.

Her lips are a duskier pink than normal. Slightly swollen. The sunset lights up her skin in a gentle rose. She looks beautiful. And very upset.

"Hello," they say quietly, and don't argue when she sits on the ledge with them.

Chapter 18

"This is a bit dangerous," Lorena says and peers down at the river.

"Yeah." They feel at once numb and electrified—like they've been kicked while they're down too many times, but it still hurts.

"Were you looking for Tallis?"

"Yeah." It comes out surprisingly bitter, and Lorena turns to them.

"We… heard you leave. *He* heard you leave… Thought it best if I… check on you."

"That wasn't necessary."

"Purcell. Just listen to me," she says sharply, and this time it's their turn to look at her in shock. "You're upset."

They think to argue but stay silent.

"Why are you sitting here? Tearing at your wrist." She points, almost touching them but pulling away at the last second.

They hold eye contact for a while, brimming with too many half-truths and no clue what to say.

Lorena shakes her head and runs out of patience.

"Are you trying to jump? Were you hoping we wouldn't catch you? I don't want to keep worrying about if you're going to just disappear one day!"

"I don't know!" Purcell finally cuts her off. "*Fuck*, I just don't *know*, oka—"

"Don't curse at me," she says lowly, and her upper lip curls like she's truly disgusted by them.

"I'm sorry." They slump over, exhausted.

The broken concrete digs into their arm, but it feels sturdy enough. The bridge shakes a little every time a car drives past behind them.

"What do we need to do for you to stop—" She points at their arm again.

Purcell closes their eyes and shakes their head. They feel underwater.

"Look at me."

They do, stunned by the moisture sticking her eyelashes together.

"*What* is wrong?"

"I don't know," they say again.

"Is it Tallis?"

"No."

"Is it me?"

"No. *Stop*. Stop," they groan and put their head back in their hands. "I just… I want to go home."

"The simulation?" she whispers and sets her hand on their back.

Purcell nods.

"What do you miss? Can you… replicate it?"

They shake their head and look at her. They're too numb to even think about the life they once had.

"No… It's gone. It's *gone*." They take a shuddering breath, and Lorena pulls her hand back. "There's nothing I can do."

"*Nothing*? At all?"

They know she means to be helpful, but the pit in their stomach keeps spreading and spreading.

They shake their head again, and it's like a bomb goes off.

Lorena is abruptly standing and starts yelling.

"God damn it, Purcell! I can't help you if you won't even help yourself! I can't keep hoping I'm going to magically say the right thing to snap you out of it! You won't even talk to me!"

They stare wide-eyed up at her, too scared to respond.

"Do you know how many questions you've asked me!?"

They're thrown by the abrupt turn.

"You keep saying we're friends, and God, I'm really trying, but you've never shown any interest in getting to know me! You don't ask me anything! You barely know me!"

They move to stand. She steps closer to block them from moving.

"Will you just get better so we can actually be happy!? How am I supposed to help you if you won't get out of your own head!?"

The barrage of questions stops like she actually wants to hear an answer.

Purcell stammers for a moment. "I don't know if—I didn't realize I was—"

Lorena glares like an apology is not what she's searching for.

Purcell finds what to say within the ache in their metal sternum, watching a mascara-greyed tear roll down her cheek.

"If... anyone could have saved me, it would have been you."

Lorena scoffs and turns away from them, toward Tallis's shed out of sight. She angrily wipes her tears and fixes them with another glare.

"You don't need *saving*, Purcell. Especially not from me." She takes a deep breath and one step back. "I can't help you."

Purcell flinches like they've been struck.

Behind her, they see another figure walking toward them—too far to discern, but they have a pretty good guess.

"I'll see you soon, Purcell." Lorena turns on her heel and storms off.

She reaches the person approaching, says something with a wide, aggressive throw of her arms, and then continues to march past.

The figure hesitates, and they can't tell if it's facing them or watching Lorena leave.

They slouch in their little alcove of broken concrete. They're watching their kickstand feet swing back and forth when the mysterious figure sits beside them.

They subtly glance to confirm—it's Tallis.

They don't react, hoping he won't talk. And he doesn't.

It's well into the night now. Every minute or so, a car's headlights will illuminate the bridge in a sweeping arc of orange.

The two sit together in silence for an hour.

The only sounds are of the frogs and crickets below, the occasional rumble of tires, and then an obnoxious beeping from Purcell's neck.

They flinch to feel for where the noise is coming from, but then everything goes black.

Chapter 19

Purcell wakes in a familiar, pastel-worn armchair. They face the blank wall without stirring, not wanting to give away that they're awake. They listen for Tallis, but there's no noise other than the birds outside and a low hum of electricity.

The songbirds lighten their mood more than they expect, and they decide to get up with a surprising lightness.

Then, they're immediately pulled down by a pressure at the back of their skull.

They yelp and fall back into the chair, reaching to pull out the cord from a wide socket in their head.

"Purcell!?" Tallis's quick footsteps sound as he jogs over.

They're still holding the cord, so they lift it and raise an eyebrow in silent question.

"You were charging. Did you close up the—" He points at their neck.

"'Close'?" Purcell pats at their neck until they find the flap that clicks into the socket to cover it.

Tallis steps back when it snaps shut.

"How did you sleep?"

"*Why* did I sleep?"

He rolls quickly with their rebuttal. "Your solar panels weren't receiving enough light, so you... shut off." He winces at the wording, but they shrug that it's fine. "But this cord is yours anyway. I was going to give it to you next time I saw you, so…"

"Thank you."

He freezes and stares at them.

Purcell thinks back to what Lorena had screamed at them last night. They force a deep breath before asking, "How was… your day?" They lean over to see out a window. It's early morning. "Yesterday," they clarify.

Tallis blinks and continues staring. "Um… It was good. How much did you… hear about? Last night."

They shake their head. "Basically nothing. Just that uh… You sent Lorena to check on me."

He nods and waits for more, but they just look at him. He has such honest, dark eyes.

His gaze darts all over their face, giving away how much he's thinking despite the silence.

"She came over for dinner yesterday," he starts, and they follow him to the kitchen. A bar stool is pushed away from the table, and several papers are stacked in front of it.

They snoop as he talks. He was reading about mutual aid societies and social media.

Tallis makes breakfast and continues the story. Lorena guessed his alumni email and messaged him the other day. They hadn't talked in a while, but they were easy friends in their classes, so it wasn't hard to reconnect.

He invited her over, and they talked all about how life has been since graduating. He'd had a crush on her when they met, but she'd been dating her ex at the time, so he hadn't approached her then.

He pauses in the retelling, so Purcell has an idea what

happened next.

They can't help the muffled laugh that escapes them. They feel well enough to joke about it though, especially after the good night's sleep.

"And then you pinned her to the wall and shoved your tongue down her throat?"

Tallis gasps and stops what he's doing to gape at them.

His jaw is dropped, and the wide-eyed stare almost makes them laugh. Eventually, he finds his words.

"Uh… no." He shakes his head and turns back to the stove. "She kissed *me*, actually, so—"

"That's not what *I* saw."

He groans and ignores them for a second to plate the food.

They watch in disbelief as he grabs a second bowl. He turns and sets it in front of them.

It's oatmeal, with sliced almonds and little pieces of straw-berry.

"We… moved," he mumbles, like it's a grave admission. "I was trying to get her to—" He mimics grabbing Lorena's waist and spinning her, then falters and looks away.

Purcell breaks and fully cackles at him. They can't believe they got him to add more detail, and clearly neither can he by how he rubs his eyes and sighs.

They can't leave it there, though, and backtrack. "What were you trying?"

He has a spoonful of oatmeal before answering. Then, he swallows hard and glances to the side. "I wanted her to sit on the counter."

"*Ah.*" Purcell nods. Lorena is short, so his reasoning makes sense. "I really cockblocked the hell out of you, huh?" They pretend to muse and lift their hand to their chin.

Tallis stammers, "No, no—We weren't—I wouldn't—Oh my God." He stabs at his oatmeal aggressively while collecting his thoughts. "No. If anything, her decision to leave was…" He fades out when they frown.

"Oh, that's right. Wasn't she—Did you carry me!?" They yell when it occurs to them.

He winces, but they're not sure for which part.

"Yes. You're fairly light, actually. One of my PREs is heavier than you." He points to one of the dog-like, rolling bots. "But um… Lorena was… She was here, talked a bit, and left."

"Did she tell you what we talked about?" Purcell hopes she didn't hash out how self-centered they've been.

"No."

They deflate with relief.

"You should eat."

Purcell blinks and looks down at their bowl.

"Sorry—Habit. But you can, anyway. It's yours."

"'Habit'? Do you have siblings?"

Tallis stills, glances up at them, then looks back down.

They sigh. This is why they don't like asking people things. They prefer staying in the freely offered information because they hate inevitably stumbling into a conversational black hole.

"No. I helped take care of… my dad. When I was younger. He was really sick."

"Oh. Is he…"

"He's dead. Died when I was fourteen."

"*God.* I'm sorry."

Tallis gives them a timid smile, and the skin around his eyes is tight.

"How old are you now?"

"24."

Purcell gasps. They guessed he was young, but his beard makes him look older than *24*.

"How old did you think I was?" He tries to joke, but that unfamiliar tension lingers.

"Oh, I don't know… Closer to my age."

He nods, then pointedly looks at their bowl and jerks his chin to encourage them.

"I think you just want to watch me eat with my weird, little pipe."

The two burst out laughing, and Purcell internally rejoices as his genuine smile returns.

He has a hint of crows' feet in the corners of his eyes, and they're looking forward to the kind wrinkles becoming more pronounced over time.

Purcell falters, and several fans in their chest start whirring.

"What?" he asks slyly.

They know their screen gave them away.

Purcell ignores him to ask instead, "What do my screen colors mean?"

He frowns. "You didn't look it up?"

"Oh." They freeze. "I didn't realize I… could."

He springs up and grabs a stapled packet from the 'Purcell table' that they identified the other day.

"Here." He flips to the right page and shows them a chart. "You're set to the North American region."

'North American Color Settings
   Red - Anger
   Orange - Surprise
   Yellow - Distress
   Green - Neutral/Calm

Blue - Sadness
Lilac- Joy
Pink - Embarrassment
Gray - Focus'

"Interesting…" They skim the other regions too. The one for China has 'Red - Joy' and 'Lilac - Embarrassment', as just a few of the differences.

"I need a new face."

Tallis chuckles and finishes the last of his breakfast. When he stands, he reaches for their bowl and raises an eyebrow.

"I'll… have some of it."

"Okay." He smiles and turns to wash just the one.

They spoon out a small amount of oatmeal and let gravity do the work.

They fully expected the food to get trapped halfway down and leave them with an uncomfortable, choking sensation, but it slides straight to their stomach.

"Oh!" They have another spoonful, and Tallis looks over his shoulder to fix them with an amused look.

"Having fun?"

"It actually goes into my stomach!"

"Where did you think it would go?" His amusement turns to concern.

"No, I'm just surprised it doesn't get stuck."

"You're lubed on the inside."

Purcell freezes and almost spills their spoonful down their front.

Tallis notices and offers an uncomfortable, wide smile that makes them laugh.

When they're done eating (only half, so he has leftovers),

Tallis takes note of their twitchy hand.

He nods to the chair, and they move to sit while he washes their bowl.

"Sorry for…" They can't bring themselves to look at him as he prepares to fix them once again.

"You don't need to apologize," he says gently, grabbing a screwdriver out of a toolbox.

He rolls his chair up and waits for them to offer their hand.

"C'mon. Let me take you apart."

They hide their flinch by shoving their hand out.

He blinks at their jumpy nature. "Does it hurt?"

"A little." They stick to the excuse, not wanting to admit that his offer pinged their brain with a fair amount of interest.

While he works, he stays more present than normal, frequently glancing at their face instead of zoning out.

"Did you move the sticker? It looks the same."

"Uh… no."

He hums like he's surprised.

"It uh…" They're scared to tank the mood, but despite the laughter and easy conversation, a permanent coldness has been waiting for them to breach it all morning. "Even though I was upset… The knowledge that it could be so easily fixed prevented me from… taking it off."

Tallis hums again, thinking. Or focusing, as he finishes and turns the sensation back on in their arm.

"Do you think that would work with other things? Like, the reasoning? If you knew how to fix everything?" He sits back and observes them closely.

Purcell holds their wrist and bends all their fingers that no longer burn. They imagine knowing how to do what he just did, but the image pivots into a terrible temptation of sinking their hand into their forearm and ripping out everything they can get a hold of.

Purcell shudders and presses their arm to their chest to stop the phantom pain.

"No," comes out harshly. "Don't tell me how to do it."

He looks startled by their begging, but he listens.

"Okay. I won't," he whispers.

A heavy silence rolls over them, and Purcell ignores his intense stare by coming up with something to say.

"Would you—" they start at the same time he says:

"What kind of—"

They nod for him to go first.

"What kind of face do you want?"

Purcell blinks. They'd assumed he thought they were joking, so the offer feels too good to be true.

They describe Eva's head to him—the blend between a human skull, but without the squishy silicone that the Sentient Robot people had.

"That sounds good," he says warmly, then nods for them to go ahead.

They build up the courage to ask again, "Would you fill out my other affidavit?"

His eyes widen, then crease into that fond eye smile.

"I'd love to."

Purcell thinks that he may be the kindest person they've ever met.

Chapter 20

Tallis shows zero judgment following Purcell into their shitty apartment. He watches them force the door closed and toes his shoes off like it's nice enough in here to do that.

"Welcome to… home?" The word falls flat, and he gives them a cute shrug that it's alright.

Having him here highlights how barren their space is. There's a single desk and chair, a bare mattress on a wooden palette, and two folders on the kitchen counter.

It's a good thing he won't be staying because it just occurred to them that they don't even own a shower curtain.

He stands at the counter and fills out the form for them. They're lucky he keeps a pen in his pocket; otherwise, they would have had to borrow one from the office downstairs.

"They really don't give us a lot of room," he mutters as he writes to the very last line. "Do you want to read it?"

"No." They hold out the folder like a shield.

He's clearly entertained, but doesn't argue as he slips the paper back in.

They snap it shut and toss it onto the counter like it was burning them.

"How are the background checks coming along?"

"In process." They hadn't noticed before, but the apartment

is so empty that louder noises echo a bit. Every time they speak, their words bounce off the bare walls.

He hums and nods like it's disappointing.

"What?"

"Just…" He looks away for a moment. "I'm worried they'll think you're older than you are."

"Oh. Is that bad?"

He shrugs. They can tell he has more to say, but they don't push.

"Thank you for…" They gesture broadly, unable to pinpoint exactly what they're feeling.

Now that they're not used to hating him, he has a very calming energy that makes them want to curl up and take a nap—barren apartment be damned.

"It's no problem." He pats the bag that he dug out of the corner of the shed—a cobweb-covered burlap bag that holds their charging cable. "You want to set this up somewhere?"

"Um…" They look at the mattress they've barely used. "Sure."

He follows their line of sight and coils up the cord by the bed. "Don't leave this plugged in unless you're actively charging, and make sure you wind it up like I just did—not by forcing it into shape, or you'll damage the wires inside, okay?"

"Okay."

He goes to the sink to rub some cobwebs off his hands, and then, to their horror, tries to turn the water on.

"The one in the bathroom—!" They try to direct him, but then he's crouched in front of the sink and trying to wedge his shoulders into the cabinet. "You don't need to—"

"It's all good," comes out muffled.

After some screechy, squeaking noise, he stands and turns on the water.

He cleans his hands, then dries them on his pants with a small, satisfied smile.

Purcell blinks in shock several times.

A crunchy, hissing noise rises from their chest as they look at Tallis. Though they're not really processing him.

They see him fixing their sink, fixing their arm, carrying them home, letting them run away, filling out the affidavit. And now, he's nervously checking them over as they continue to hiss with static.

Purcell lurches forward to hug him, and he freezes for only a moment before recovering and wrapping his arms around them.

"I'm sorry," they whisper. "Thank you for… everything. Even though it's been… difficult… Thank you for waking me up."

They feel his sharp inhale, and it makes them want to cry. There's too much nervous energy in them to do so, but their core aches like they're crying regardless.

"I'm sorry it was so hard on you," he whispers and rests his chin on their shoulder. "I wish I'd known at the time how to help you… instead of… leaving you to yourself."

Purcell steps back to see his face, but they keep their hands on his shoulders to remain grounded.

"I'm sorry for taking it out on you."

He gives them a sad, crooked smile that brings attention to how he's holding back his own tears.

"It's okay."

They pull him back into the hug, and he steps closer this time to really envelop them. They rock side to side a bit and daydream about how lucky they are that he was the one to wake them.

"I'm sorry Lorena is…" He fades out, and they sigh.

"It's understandable," they admit. "I just hate making people cry. I feel… cruel."

Tallis flinches and steps away. "*No*, please, you're—Don't put so much pressure on yourself."

His wide eyes make them realize that there's something wrong with what they said, but they're not sure what it was.

"You're not *cruel*. Sometimes people just… react. You can't always know when… someone's going to break. Don't blame it on yourself."

They nod, but he keeps going.

"Don't blame it on her either. I think she's… I think there are many small things piling up that made her so angry last night. Not just…"

"Me?"

He hesitates but then nods.

They sigh and reluctantly agree, but still feel the need to explain their thought process.

"If I'm… If I'm making the people around me unhappy, then… what's even the point of me being here?"

Tallis's expression crumbles as his eyes water fully this time. He cups their little, rectangular head in his hands and scans their face like he's searching for something.

They didn't realize their words would cause such a reaction, and they wait for some groundbreaking statement from him. But instead, he gently pulls them forward and presses his lips to the top of their head.

"I worry about you."

They stand back up straight and watch him wipe his tears away.

"Sorry."

He laughs pitifully and shrugs. "It comes with the territory," he jokes, and they find themselves smiling with him despite the pain in their chest.

"Taking care of me?"

He nods but clarifies, "Taking care of friends… Fixing you up for those few months was… good for me too." He winces and adds, "Sorry my example is before you were even awake, but having you was genuinely very helpful for… that time."

They frown at his apology, not thinking anything bad before.

"What was going on?" Purcell asks.

He runs a hand through his hair and holds the back of his neck as he puts words together.

"I…" He sighs, and they're about to tell him not to worry about it when it all spills out at once. "I think my purpose is to take care of people. It makes me feel needed. It gets me out of bed in the morning." He looks out the window, and the sunlight shines through his eyes like a whiskey bottle.

"Before you… I went too long alone—not really… helping anything or feeling like I was doing any good in the world."

They flinch when they consider how much their anger at him must have hurt.

"Those six months, although unknowingly, helping a person again was… really fulfilling for me." He smiles, and his tone curls into amusement. "You also helped me get out of debt because everything I learned about robotics while repairing you became really applicable to my career."

Purcell snorts and jokes, "Really? Repairing a robot helped you repair robots? What a shocker."

"Oh. I guess I've never—Do you know what my job is?"

They hesitate. "Is it not…"

"I code and repair PREs for people—usually kids."

"Oh." They feel like the scum of the earth. Lorena was

completely justified in lecturing them on how oblivious they are to the people in their life.

"You're blue," Tallis whispers and slowly reaches for a hand.

They take his and squeeze his fingers in an attempt to be reassuring.

"Can you like… adamantly make me pull my head out of my ass when—"

His startled laughter cuts them off briefly.

"You know what I mean. I don't know if Lorena mentioned it, but I'm sorry for literally never asking you questions ever. I don't know why I'm like this."

"Let's make a deal."

Purcell frowns, but nods for him to continue.

"We can't apologize anymore today, and let bygones be bygones. It's just time to be… better versions of ourselves from now on."

They scoff. "I don't know if you can get any better."

He frowns like they've gravely insulted him, then surprises them with, "I could argue that you were doing fine as well because you were in such a strange, horrifying situation all on your own. I never… It's unreasonable to expect… You did your best, is what I'm trying to say. I never took anything you did personally because it was so clear how distressing just… existing was at first."

They feel washed in his words for several seconds.

"Thank you."

He smiles like they've said something funny.

"And I'm glad. I'm glad you didn't take any of the shit I said seriously, 'cause—"

"Hey, that's not what I said," he teases.

"You know what I mean."

He shrugs it off, then glances out the window again. They follow his gaze, looking at the building beside them and a triangle of cloudy sky.

"How has…" he starts, and Purcell turns to look at his side profile. "How has the… world differed from the simulations so far?" He turns to them, but his eyes are glazed like he isn't really looking at them.

"Um… There's been a lot," they admit. "People are really different. Including… me."

"Yeah?" He shifts his weight like he wants to sit down, and they make a mental note to start actually furnishing and living in their apartment.

"In the simulation… people were—I had friends, but they never surprised me. We weren't… super close, and I honestly preferred to be alone because… it felt the same. People were predictable. And not particularly interesting."

"And that's different from here?" he jokes.

"*Yes.*" They playfully roll their eyes.

"That makes sense then."

"Hm?"

"Why you were so distant."

"Oh… Yeah, I guess." They look down at their hands. They open and close them several times, still unnerved by how numb they are. "I miss my piano though."

"'Piano'?" He tilts his head. "Oh, that's right," he says at the same time they ask:

"Did you read—"

He nods.

"Yeah," they say lamely gland let their arms fall by their sides.

"Is that the first thing you're going to put in this apartment?" he teases them, and they huff a disbelieving laugh at him. For how kind he is normally, he's still observant enough to use his skills to be annoying.

"Not intentionally, but yeah. A keyboard might be the first thing I buy. Or loan? I don't know."

"Yeah. I meant to ask if you were planning on getting a job. You can do most without proof of sentience."

"I have no idea." They look out the window and imagine doing a random customer service job. "I don't think that would go well actually."

"No?" He sounds genuinely surprised.

"No. I don't have much patience for people."

"Well," he laughs. "That does make it hard."

They try to scrunch their nose at him, but they have no idea how it translates on their screen face. "Being a student might be a lot on its own anyway."

"Oh! Are you wanting to—"

"For piano." They have to force the words out. "I don't... have my muscle memory anymore."

His eyes widen, and they're silently pleased to see hurt in them. "Wow, that's... I mean... Good luck?" he offers weakly. "That sounds really time-consuming, but as long as you enjoy it...?"

"Yeah. It's the thing I miss the most, I think."

"Speaking of which." He stands up straight, and they subconsciously copy him. "Did you want to reach out to Lorena? I know how stubborn she is, and unfortunately... she tends to just... stew. She's not going to reach out first."

"Really?" They wince.

"Yeah," he says like he doesn't want to insult her but can't lie either. "You don't have to, but..."

"I want to resolve things. I... feel bad for pushing her away."

He nods. "I can text her now if you want. Is her affidavit notarized?"

"Yeah."

"Oh. Damn, you guys are fast."

They hold in their laughter and watch him pull out his phone.

"Well… That was going to be my excuse," he explains.

"You can be blunt instead. I don't mind."

"Tell her you feel guilty and to please come over to hear you apologize?" he jokes, but they nod. "Okay. I'll type it in better words."

"Thank you." They anxiously shift their weight back and forth, and when that's not enough, they start pacing.

"Are you going to be okay?"

"Would you practice with me?" rushes out of them.

"Your apology?"

"Yeah."

He smiles and pockets his phone. "Sure."

They spend several minutes practicing, and Lorena is on her way already.

Oddly, she asks if she can bring Corey with her, and Purcell has Tallis text that that would be delightful.

Purcell makes him listen as they prepare line after line of excuses until eventually giving up. Their wholly unprepared when she texts that she's at their building.

Tallis goes downstairs to lead her up, and Purcell panics in their apartment alone. They feel like they're going to throw up, and they hope that isn't something they can do.

Tallis knocks quietly before opening the door, and Purcell steps out of the bathroom to see all three of them.

Chapter 21

"Hi?" Lorena greets first and positions the stroller between herself and Purcell like a little barrier.

"Hi," they sigh and practically deflate seeing her face.

She wiggles the stroller into the kitchen and hovers just outside of Purcell's reach.

"I'm *so* sorry. Thank you for yelling at me 'cause I really needed it, and I was—"

Lorena throws herself at them, and the bear hug almost knocks them over. "Needed or not, *I'm* sorry. I felt so terrible; I couldn't sleep at all last night. I can't believe I just left you there! I don't know what I was—"

"You're okay. I wasn't alone after all."

"But still, it was irrespons—"

"It's like you said. It was mean of me to *make* you feel responsible in the first—"

"Oh, but it wasn't your fault. That's just how I am." Lorena sighs, and Purcell shrugs with a timid smile.

Lorena turns to glance at Corey, and Tallis is cooing over the stroller. He looks up when he feels eyes on him, and smiles awkwardly at being caught.

She turns to Purcell when they speak a little quieter. "Why are you… I'm curious now. Why are you so… soldier-y?"

"'Soldier'?" Lorena frowns.

"You're all, 'I can carry the weight of everyone on my shoulders.'" They try to be funny, but their concern makes it land too heavily.

"I… My ex was…" She gestures loosely back at Corey. "He—" Her voice cracks.

Purcell opens their arms, and she gladly accepts the invitation. She thunks her forehead right against their sternum.

"What happened? With your ex?" Purcell asks and watches as Tallis fights not to look at them. He keeps his eyes on Corey, but he looks sad.

"He killed himself," Lorena whispers.

Purcell flinches and tightens their arms around her.

"We weren't… on speaking terms. We had already been separated for… months. But…" She sighs and lifts onto her toes to rest her chin on Purcell's shoulder.

"I'm sorry."

"It's okay. It's not why I'm telling you, I just…" She steps back and rubs her face. "I'm tired. I don't want to… fight someone about it again."

They fill in the blanks. "I'm sorry for scaring you."

She gives them a watery smile, but the genuine light behind her eyes tells them she forgives them.

Tallis leans against the kitchen counter. He doesn't look surprised.

Purcell wonders if Lorena got angry at them for being so uncaring after speaking with him yesterday. They couldn't be more different from him—open and warm and thoughtful. Talking to Tallis is probably the easiest way to realize how inconsiderate they are in comparison.

"I'm sorry again for—"

She tries to wave them off, but they catch her hand and stay serious.

"No, listen."

Her wide eyes sharpen, so they know they're on thin ice.

"I appreciate you. I want to know more about you. I don't know how to—I still want to hear from you. Hear *about* you. I'm not… I wasn't going to…" They stare and hope she understands what they can't say.

She smiles and squeezes their fingers. They feel it because the pistons in their arm shift as their fingers move.

They both look when Corey babbles nonsensical sounds at Tallis.

"Does she like you?" Lorena asks. "She'll reach out and try to grab you if she does."

"Then… I think so."

"Mama!" Corey yells for the first time as Lorena steps into view.

"Baby!" She cheers back, and Purcell clutches over their heart.

They move to wipe tears and accidentally smack their glass really hard. The others look up at the *thunk*, and it startles Purcell so badly that they feel like they reset.

Seeing the three all happy and together finally makes them cry. And they rush to hide in the bathroom.

"Oh, *Purcell!*" Lorena admonishes them for running and hugs them. Even though she's so much tinier than Tallis, she holds them much tighter.

They sob into her hair for a minute.

"I didn't realize you could cry, honey." She rubs their back and murmurs sweet words while waiting.

"Thank you," they groan when they get their breathing under

control. "A lot has happened these past few days."

"Ugh, yeah."

They don't like how quickly she can relate, but they don't pry.

Tallis pokes his head in, and Purcell squeezes hard before letting go.

"Do you want to go out for lunch while we get the other form signed?" he asks.

"Sure! If you don't mind the company." She bounces on her toes.

Purcell agrees too, and they search for a nearby notary on the computer.

"Oh." They have an email.

"Oh?" Lorena peers over their shoulder, then gasps and grabs them to near-violently shake around, cheering.

Tallis comes to loom over their other shoulder. "Oh, perfect," he says lowly when they click to the second message as well.

Both background checks cleared.

"If I print them now, we can—"

"County clerk?"

"*Yeah*." Purcell turns to look at him. "How do you know that?"

He flushes, and Lorena stifles her laugh.

"I… researched the process when you told me you were doing it."

"That's… thorough," they mumble, instead of any number of compliments they could have chosen.

The office downstairs lets Purcell print for free.

Then, the three postpone lunch to go to a notary and the county clerk's office before they close.

Tallis has to wait outside because he has a knife in his pocket, and Lorena decides to wait with him after Purcell reassures her that they'll be okay.

They get a pat-down beside the metal detector, and then they spend a few minutes wandering around, reading signs, and taking an elevator to find the Special Proceedings desk. There's no line, and the woman working is very quick and professional.

"Your court date is written here. Bring all your documents with you because if you pass, we'll need it to register you, and if you fail, you'll need it all to refile the case if you want." She slides a copy of their Notice of Intent of Proof of Sentience and their background checks back.

"Okay. Thank you so much." They stuff everything back into their folder.

The woman smiles for the first time. "You're welcome, and good luck."

"Thank you." Purcell smiles back, then rushes to rejoin the two outside.

Tallis is leaning back against a pillar, watching Lorena animatedly talk, with a warm look on his face. He catches Purcell's eye and stands up straight like he doesn't want to get caught basking in her attention.

She notices and turns to yell, "How'd it go?"

"It was good! I wasn't missing anything, and the court date is in five days."

"Nice!" Lorena bounces on the balls of her feet, and Corey babbles at the sound of her mom so excited.

Tallis's gaze softens even more, looking at them both, and Purcell bumps against his side to subtly tease him about it.

He huffs, but hides it by asking, "So… lunch? Early dinner?"

"*Please*. I'm starving," Lorena whines.

No one has objections to the first restaurant they pass, so they enter a taco place that's fairly busy for 4 p.m.

The host tries to talk Tallis into a two-person table that's clear, but he clarifies that they can wait for three people.

"The robot's yours?" they ask him, and Tallis folds and answers:

"Yes."

"Alright. Give us a second to clear a table, and I'll call you over."

"Okay, thanks." Tallis nods and moves to a corner before getting close to mutter, "Sorry."

Purcell laughs, and his tense shoulders fall.

"I don't mind. It is funny though that—"

"Tallis?" A waiter introduces himself and leads them to a table.

"What was funny?" Lorena asks when they're seated.

"Oh. I was just gonna say it's funny you apologized because I know *I* don't mind, but I met a group of robots a while ago that would've gotten *so* offended by it. It's just…" They shake their head, smiling at the mental image of the Sentient Meeting robots being asked if their human friends owned them.

Lorena stifles her laugh at the explanation, like she's unsure if she's allowed to find it funny or not.

"Well, to be fair—" Tallis gets interrupted by the waiter coming back to take everyone's order.

When they're alone again, Purcell nods for him to continue, but he hesitates.

"What? Playing devil's advocate?" they joke.

He crunches his nose in distaste, which they've never seen him do before. It makes him look almost his age.

"Definitely not. I was…" He sighs and spins his glass of water like it's the most interesting thing in the world.

Lorena leans to bump shoulders, and it pulls him back to the present.

"I was just going to say that some humans like feeling owned too."

Lorena sputters as she drinks water at the inopportune time, and she chokes on her laughter while Purcell is similarly stunned by his surprisingly lewd joke.

"Jeez, Tallis," they mutter and feel their fans kick up a notch. He smiles like a grimace and sips his water.

"I'd like to make it clear—" They start, but Lorena is too quick and starts giggling, at *their* expense this time. "Dear, they're really going to think we're all high or something." They tease her, and she even laughs through her apology.

"God, I *feel* high." She wipes her tears and forces herself to calm down.

Purcell backtracks to joke so Tallis will relax. "But I really do want to make it clear that I don't mind because it's *convenient*. Not because I'm overly fond of being another robot pet of yours."

Tallis huffs a laugh and nods.

"Only slightly fond then?" Lorena jabs with a cute, impish grin.

Purcell shrugs it off, and finally Tallis's smile loses its tense shadow.

The rest of dinner passes easily, and Purcell finds it difficult to say goodbye that evening.

Chapter 22

Purcell practices on their keyboard the morning of their court hearing.

Tallis took them to buy it on the same day Lorena showed up with a few random apartment supplies, so their home feels more lived in.

They don't own a dresser, so they keep their few articles of clothing piled beside the keyboard. Occasionally, they move them to cover up the keys when they can't stand to look at it without crying.

They've mostly been practicing the scales and chipping away one note at a time to relearn songs by ear. It's almost relaxing, but today, there isn't much they can do to stave off the anxiety of the sentience test in a few hours.

The keyboard's lowest volume is still a bit loud, and they feel bad for their neighbors having to listen to their poor playing.

Tallis is waiting for pieces to arrive before he can install pressure-sensitive hands to them, so they're relying completely on sight to hit the correct keys. It's incredibly tedious, and it makes them play extra slow, but the satisfaction every time they get to the end of a song motivates them further.

At 10 a.m., they leave for their court hearing at 11.

Lorena is waiting outside, wearing a long white dress with a button-up shirt over it. Her hair is wavy like she curled it this morning, and she has makeup on that makes her look rosy and warm.

She greets Purcell with a big hug and rocks side to side. "Are you excited?"

"Nervous."

"Oh, you'll do fine." She pats their arms, and Tallis appears from behind a pillar, hanging up his phone.

He's wearing a white shirt under an off-white button-up that matches off-white pants. It's the first time Purcell has ever seen him not wearing jeans, and he even trimmed his scruff a bit so it has cleaner lines.

They're glad the clothes they bought with Lorena are fairly nice. Otherwise, the twos' cleaned-up appearances would really make them stand out. And not in a good way.

Although acting pitiful might be a good approach for the hearing.

"Are you ready to go in?" Tallis asks softly, and Purcell looks away to pretend they haven't been staring.

"I think so… Thank you both for coming."

"Of course, hon! This is fun anyway. It's the only time I'll ever come to court with no stress," Lorena jokes and stands by Tallis.

There's a strange energy between them when she moves closer. He shifts his weight toward her, and their arms brush like they can't help it.

Purcell narrows their eyes, and Lorena flushes and looks away. Tallis smiles as her reaction gives the two away.

Now that Purcell sees them next to each other, it becomes really clear that the blue shirt Lorena is wearing is Tallis's size.

"Did you…"

Lorena gives them a deer-in-headlights look.

"Did you… come here together?"

"Yeah," Tallis answers, and he serenely looks at Lorena as she sputters. "I spent the night at her apartment." He turns back to Purcell and shrugs. "So I didn't have to make the long walk this morning."

"*Ah.* That's good." They try to stay professional, but their façade breaks when they snort and feel their sides sputter with laughter.

"We didn't sleep together," he adds, but it makes Lorena grab his arm like she wants to pull him away to stop talking.

"I never said you did."

"You didn't have to," he jokes back, and Lorena starts screeching like an upset seagull.

He yanks the arm in her grasp, so she falls with it to crash into his side. Then he turns to whisper something into her hair, and she relaxes from whatever it is.

The two follow Purcell into the courthouse this time. They go through the metal detector, but Purcell gets another pat-down.

After examining a floor plan, they find the room where the hearing will take place and sit on a bench outside it. The two sit on either side of Purcell, who's almost vibrating from the stress.

Tallis is texting someone, and when they glance at the screen, it's a long thread of technical jargon for PRE specifications.

Lorena is slumped back with her eyes closed, and they would think she was asleep if she wasn't rhythmically tapping each of their knuckles on the hand that she pulled into her lap.

"Purcell?" A stranger pokes their head out of the room, then props the door open when they jump to stand. "And two witnesses?"

"Yes."

"Y'all can come on in."

All three follow to enter a much smaller room than they expected. It kind of feels like one of the library's study rooms. It's also completely empty.

Purcell frantically scans before sitting to the right, facing the judge's empty spot.

Lorena sits between them and Tallis, and they ask to check the time on her phone.

10:58.

They release a deep breath and clutch their shaking hands to their screen mouth.

Lorena laughs and pets the back of their head. "You're gonna be okay, hon. Promise."

"'Promise'?" They turn to her with an impressed, arched eyebrow. "That's brave."

She smiles, and they all flinch when footsteps sound from a room beside them.

Three people enter from a doorway at the front, and two weasel out from behind the judge's chair.

Purcell watches with wide eyes as the judge sits down.

"Good morning! How are y'all doing?"

"Good!" Purcell squeaks out. They feel like their fans are going to shoot them into the sky. "And you?"

"I'm doing well! Thank you!" He smiles wide, then gestures to the two others. "This is Dr. Fujimoto. She'll be assessing you on your sentience while we talk. Just act normal. Don't worry. And this is—"

"Luca." The man waves, and Purcell nods back.

They're too shocked by everyone's warmth to move.

"He'll be guiding the conversation, and if you do well, he'll also be the one to fill out your SSN."

"SSN?" Purcell whispers to Lorena.

"Social Security Number," she whispers back quickly.

"Ah. Okay." They nod and look back and forth between the table beside them and the judge.

The doctor is already writing with a small smile. She has bright green hair, and it continually slides from behind her ear to drape over her face.

Luca is less flashy, but he feels just as approachable with his warm demeanor. She whispers something to him, and he nods before addressing Purcell.

When he speaks, they see the tooth gems flash on his canines. "Do you have a Cloud server for your conscious data?"

"Uh… no."

"Not at all? Can you reach the internet in any way from your physical servers?"

"No."

Luca whispers something to Fujimoto.

Tallis tentatively raises his hand, and the judge nods for him to speak.

"Hi. I'm Purcell's… engineer? I fix them up, I mean, and uh… their model is so old that they don't actually have the capacity to access the internet. They'd have to install hardware for it first."

"Ah, okay. That's cool! I've actually never run across that before," Luca admits. "Now, if you wouldn't mind… Who are both the people with you?"

Purcell leans back so he can see and points. "My two witnesses who wrote the affidavit forms for me. Lorena, a friend. And Tallis, also a friend, but… also my mechanic."

The two give very brief descriptions of how they met Purcell, and luckily, Luca doesn't ask for clarification on the "woke them out of a simulation" thing.

When the two are done, Purcell remembers a random thing they could have checked off on the court form and adds, "And neither of them are here by subpoena. They came here… of their own accord."

Luca frowns, and for a terrible second, they think they've said something wrong.

"Neither are?" He repeats.

"Yeah. I mean, *yes*, they aren't."

"No, I got that. It's grammatically correct to say 'neither is'."

Purcell blinks, almost offended, but they're too confused. "I'm… sorry?"

"No, this is good." He gives them a thumbs-up as Fujimoto nods and flips a paper to check something off.

"Okay. This is the weirdest part of the test." Luca prefaces and stands. "Please, tell me what's wrong with this image." He presents a sheet of paper, and Purcell squints through the immediate headache it causes.

"You mean other than the fact that it's moving?" They try not to whine, but the eye strain is really uncomfortable. The spiral of clashing lines and colors squirms around despite being printed.

"Great. Thank you." Luca returns to his table and hovers beside Fujimoto as she talks lowly and flips through a packet.

They strain to eavesdrop (politeness at the bottom of their list of cares after the weird grammar correction) and catch him say, "—need much more. Do you want to ask anything?"

She answers, but it's too quiet.

Luca sits down and speaks to the judge. "We're passing with

flying colors so far. Do you mind if we switch to the legal side now?"

The judge opens his hands to gesture openly. "Not at all. You two are the experts here."

"Okay," Fujimoto speaks for the first time. She turns to look at Purcell, and they follow suit, trying not to stare too hard at the long strip of creamy skin exposed by the slit in her dress.

"I'd like it if you could tell me why you're seeking proof of sentience, Purcell."

They blink, fully obsessed with this beautiful, intelligent woman who said their name so charmingly. She has a hint of a tattoo on her upper thigh, and her legs are *so* long. They wonder how high up the tattoo goes on her side.

"Um…"

Tallis makes a weird, muffled noise behind them, and Purcell flushes when it clicks that he's trying not to laugh.

"Please. It's okay if you're not sure," she adds.

"Right." They haul their thoughts to the task at hand. "I… want to attend Kim's Music School. And I tried to apply but… they wanted proof of sentience, so… yeah."

Fujimoto nods and writes something, subtly nodding along.

An alarm goes off, and Purcell flinches as Luca apologizes and silences his phone.

"Excellent." She checks one last thing, then stands. "I'll need all three of you to sign these, and then, Your Honor, if you would please sign Purcell's order."

"Gladly," he says as their eyes widen.

"I—Did I—"

"You passed." She smiles, and Lorena squeals and grabs Purcell's arm to shake them around.

"Oh, thank *God*."

Everyone in the room smiles as the weight visibly lifts off their shoulders.

The three sign NDAs that they won't disclose the steps of the sentience test online or with anyone not present, and then Luca guides Purcell through the Social Security application.

"Cool." He closes the file. "I'll send this, and then you'll receive your card in the mail in about 2 weeks. So don't move, okay?"

"Alright."

"This is yours," Fujimoto says as well, and hands them the stapled papers that had the checklist. "You don't have to keep it. But if you were curious." She shrugs.

"Oh, thank you! I kind of am." They flip through it, barely skimming before deciding to save it for later.

"And remember, you have legal sentience, but not personhood. They're two different things."

Purcell stalls, not having read about that before. Their eyes widen, hoping she isn't about to crush their spirit with news that they haven't actually accomplished anything today.

"Personhood is the next step if you want, but it isn't necessary for most schools or businesses. It's only required if you want to adopt, get married, teach, things like that."

"Oh. What's the… process for it?"

"It's similar." Fujimoto smiles like she wants to soften the blow but can't. "The hardest thing is a list of your residences and workplaces from the last 10 years. We would also need a formal statement from you regarding what your intentions are to file for personhood specifically. It's harder to attain legally, although I think you have it regardless. You would have an easy time passing."

"Oh…" They nod. "I don't think I'll… worry about that just

yet."

"Okay. Just remember to write important dates down so the process is easier in the future."

"Um. I will." They don't know if they'll ever want to deal with filing for personhood, but it was nice of her to mention it.

Fujimoto nods politely, then turns back to Luca.

"Thank you," they say loudly to the room in general, then join Tallis and Lorena by the door.

"Congratulations!" the judge yells before they leave.

Purcell waves, then walks out.

Chapter 23

Lorena and Tallis accompany them to the piano school, and they sign up with no problems.

There's a different person working the front desk, and the sentience number on their certificate was the only thing missing from last time.

They sign up for a Tuesday-Thursday class with a Miss Flores, and receive a plastic card that they can scan to enter the practice rooms at any time.

"Lunch to celebrate?" Lorena asks.

"Don't you work today?" Purcell reminds her, hoping it isn't rude.

"I took the day off."

"Oh."

"We should do something grander to celebrate you though, when we're all free. Do you like the beach? I haven't been to Greenville in a long time," she offers.

"I… don't know," they admit. "I don't know if sand is a good idea actually." They gesture to their many exposed joints.

"Oh, that's true."

The two turn to Tallis, who's once again on the phone, talking to someone about a pick-up later that week for their newly upgraded PRE. He confirms a time, thanks them, hangs up, and then presumably enters the date on his calendar.

Finally, he turns to the two and says, "I heard 'lunch'. Is that what we're doing?"

Lorena giggles like she finds everything he does endearing, and Purcell considers teasing them as they once again gravitate toward each other.

They lead the way back toward the city center, looking for open restaurants. They faintly hear Tallis ask if he can hold her hand, and Lorena squeaks an affirmative.

They turn into a 'Jerusalem Spot' restaurant that looks good, and the three are seated inside.

"Can I look at the test when you're done?" Tallis asks as they're waiting on their food.

"Oh yeah." Purcell pulls the packet out to properly read.

It's relatively short, with only eight questions. It looks longer because each section has a paragraph on why it's important and how to quantify it.

The sections are 'Sentient Witnesses, Response Time, Reasonable Hostility, Attention Span, Startle Response, Visual Perception, Language Dynamism, and Intention'.

"Here." Purcell hands it to Tallis, and Lorena reads over his shoulder.

"This is *really* interesting..." he mumbles and reads much more thoroughly. "Can I take a photo of this? I want to read more on—"

"Yeah, yeah. Don't worry." They wave loosely for him to do whatever.

"Thanks." He photographs each page, and then their food comes out.

While they're eating (including Purcell as they sip a lentil soup), Tallis casually says, "I bet Corey would like all the lights in here."

Lorena stills, then looks at him with wide eyes. She has sauce smeared at the corner of her lips, and it takes everything within them not to reach out and wipe it off, but that's presumably Tallis's job now.

Purcell buries the small coal of resentment and tries to watch their interaction with a forced calmness. They missed some of it, but Lorena is baffled that he didn't mind navigating downtown with the baby and stroller.

"I try not to take her everywhere. She can be so noisy."

"It's alright though. You shouldn't feel limited just because she might cry. It's important to still get out and go places. Otherwise, you could harbor little pieces of anger over time for feeling like she's stopping you from having fun."

"Oh, but I know it isn't her fault," Lorena argues.

"That's good! But do you wish she could be left alone more?"

"Of course."

Tallis smirks like he's won, and Lorena pouts when she realizes it.

"I guess... I see... how that could lead to a bad place."

He nods and keeps eating.

He still chews cutely, like a squirrel with big bites. Purcell distracts themselves by sipping more of their soup.

"All I'm saying is... I hope you trust that you can bring Corey out with you more." Tallis glances between them. "And I hope you're happy."

Lorena smiles and bumps their sides together.

Tallis looks pointedly at Purcell too, and they nod as well.

After lunch, the three part ways. Lorena and Tallis are going to her mother's to get Corey, and Purcell heads back to the piano school to practice before classes start next week.

They find an empty practice room and clunk away at their scales.

A light knock startles them into looking up, and a man with fluffy, blond hair leans in like he's checking on them.

"Hi! Didn't want to spook you." He comes in and sets up a few stands in the back of the room.

They watch him curiously, so he explains. "The younger kids have a performance tomorrow. We're gonna be sending the recording to all the parents."

"Ah. That's cute." Purcell nods and timidly keeps practicing.

"I'm Uriel, by the way. They/them. I'm one of the teachers—mostly keyboard and violin."

"Cool. I'm uh… brand new." They cringe saying that, but move on. "Purcell."

"Nice to meet you!" They smile blindingly before finishing the setup for the video. "Who are you learning under?"

"Uh…" They can't remember and look at their card in the hope that her name is on it.

"Violet? Flores? Sykes?" he offers.

"Ah! Yes, Flores."

Uriel chuckles, then bids them good luck before leaving them alone again.

Purcell keeps practicing.

After an indeterminable amount of time, the frustration of their senseless fingers drives them to angrily pace the room.

They find a techniques book for beginners propped on another keyboard and grab it to use while they're here. They start at page one and play exercise after exercise until everything starts to sound the same.

There's no clock in the room, so they have no idea how long they've been here. They get the feeling it's been a while, especially when Uriel gasps in the doorway.

Purcell graciously accepts the distraction and stands up to stretch.

"Hi."

"Hi!? You've been here hours! Are you—How's it going?"

Purcell snorts at their distress and continues stretching their back. "It's good. I think I'm gonna head home now anyway."

"Goodness. Well, make sure you rest, alright?"

"I will, I will." Purcell waves off their concern and collects their things. "Good luck with the—" They gesture at the camera setup.

"Thank you! I'm sure we'll bump into each other again," Uriel says and backs out into the hallway.

"Yep! Good night!" Purcell heads out after seeing the dark sky through the glass doors. They hadn't noticed until now, but there are no windows in the practice room either. They should probably invest in a watch so they don't lose track of time in there.

Not that that would be a bad thing. They desperately need to improve if they want to feel good about themselves.

This is the last piece from their previous life that they're missing, and it feels out of reach with their current body.

For the first time though, Purcell would rather stay and figure it out than travel back to live the life that they had before.

Chapter 24

"I wanted to wring her fuckin' neck," Purcell grumbles and mimes doing exactly that around their mug.

Lorena's eyebrows raise as she takes a sip of her tea.

"But I settled for just calling her a cunt."

Lorena spews tea everywhere, and several eyes turn to them as she sputters and exclaims, "Oh my God! Purcell!"

They playfully pat her back, but she swats at them until they laugh.

"Sorry."

Lorena shakes her head, then rubs her eyes and lets out a deep breath. "Honey, I love you, but you really need to be careful now that you can get in trouble."

Purcell barely registers anything after *I love you*, and freezes for a moment too long to go unnoticed.

Lorena smiles and sighs. "You know, I asked Tallis what all your screen colors mean the other night."

They blink in surprise, but nod for her to go on.

"You're not gonna blue screen on me, but I worry you're gonna turn pink and shut off one day," she jokes.

Purcell weakly whines in response.

"But really, hon. Now that you have sentience... As much as I love your... *assertive* personality."

They snort but don't interrupt.

Corey babbles from the stroller, and Lorena bends down to pick up the toy she threw on the ground.

"I don't want you to be paranoid, but you *are* more likely to legitimately get in trouble now. So... no wringing necks allowed."

"I know, that's why I—Oh. Sorry. I didn't even realize—" They reach as if to cover Corey's ears in retrospect.

"It's okay. Just don't say it again so she doesn't learn it."

Purcell frantically nods, then leans down to look at her. "*Cup.* I said *cup*, sweet girl."

Lorena smiles as Corey squeals and reaches for them.

Purcell gives her their pinky to hold, and she babbles happily while swinging their hands.

"But no, I promise," they backtrack and look up at Lorena. "I'll do my best to be... well, not *nice*, but—"

She laughs at the disclaimer. "I know what you mean. And I'm sorry she said that to you. Although I'm happy for you that you're improving so quickly that you can even be *accused* of cheating your way through."

"I *know*. Flores even backed me up and said that anyone who stayed after to practice as much as me would be doing just as well—robot or not."

"I just wish there was another robot in your class."

"Yeah, me too. Although..."

Corey lets go of their pinky, so they sit up.

"Other robots are really hit or miss. Some of them are *so* annoying," Purcell groans and tilts their head back.

Someone laughs behind them, and they worry they're being eavesdropped on. They quiet down a little and hope it's unrelated.

Lorena must notice too because she changes the subject, a bit quieter.

Eventually, they circle back to piano. "Are you free Thursday night?"

"Um… What time?"

"Starts at six."

"Oh, then yeah." She nods but tilts her head.

"It's our first mini concert."

Her eyes widen, and she gasps before excitedly grabbing their hands. "That's so exciting! Have you invited Tallis?"

"Not yet."

"What about True and Eva?"

"Uh… no." They saw them again last weekend, but they're still not feeling close enough to any of the robots to invite them out to other places.

Lorena rolls her eyes at Purcell's clear favoritism among their friends. "Well, I'll be there for sure! Is it everyone performing?"

"Everyone in my class, yeah."

She squeezes their fingers before letting go to finish the last of her tea.

"I still can't believe you don't like coffee."

She giggles and sets her cup down. "I can't *help* it. Caffeine makes my head hurt." She pouts.

They finish their drink too, then walk with her. They nervously scan the shop before leaving to see that the person who laughed behind them is a familiar-looking robot.

For a second, Purcell thinks they're from the Sentient Robots' meeting, but that doesn't feel quite right. It's only when they look at the woman they're sitting with that it clicks.

The two have their hands overlapped on the table, and the woman has lesbian-flag-colored wisteria earrings. She's giving her robot partner the most palpable heart eyes Purcell has ever seen, and they remember standing behind the two in line the day they met Lorena.

"Everything okay?" Lorena reaches to tug Purcell's arm.

A stranger is holding the door for her to get through with the stroller.

"Ah, yes! Thank you!" They rush through after her. "Just… got distracted."

They spend the next few hours in Lorena's apartment, playing block games with Corey and watching cheesy soap operas.

When it's time to go home, Purcell daydreams about their fellow student who accused them of faking their progress in class. They hope she doesn't come to the concert later this week, but they find that, after talking with Lorena, her comments don't sting as much as before.

Chapter 25

The day before the concert, Purcell spends hours in the practice room. They have one song to perform, and their confidence fluctuates every time they play it. Sometimes they play it perfectly. Sometimes they mess up at the very first line.

Since they're in the beginners' class, they don't need to memorize the piece. They've discovered that with how many times they've played it, they've memorized it anyway.

Students are supposed to use the practice room keyboards with earbuds, but Purcell doesn't have inner ears. They asked Miss Flores if she'd like them to buy over-the-ear headphones, but the practice rooms are never full, so instead they just play audibly. Anyone who needs silence can use another room.

They feel a bit guilty when people peek in just to leave, but it's not so bad. They've found it especially helpful when the instructor can easily give feedback after simply passing by.

"Make sure you slow down the ending." Flores greets them warmly.

"Oh yeah. Thank you." Purcell plays it again, slowing down the last two bars.

"Very good."

"Thank you!"

"I heard you in the hall. You've been here longer than normal."

"Ah… yeah."

"You should rest for tomorrow. You'll have plenty of time to practice during class beforehand as well." She holds out a plastic container, and they stand to see what's inside.

It's full of little slices of cake.

Purcell gasps and takes a cube. "Oh, they're so cute!"

The endless frustration from trying to be as good as they remember lightens in the face of dessert.

Playing piano is so much harder here than it was in their head, and they've found themselves repeatedly trying not to miss their simulation lifestyle. And it's small, kind gestures like these that confirm over and over that the people in this life are more important than all the fame and comfortable success that they miss.

Flores watches with alarm as Purcell whirrs loudly before getting shaky breathing like they're going to cry.

They explain that they're okay and that their crying is normal before showing her how the piece of cake plops into their intake tube for them to eat.

"Ta-da. It's here now." Purcell points at the freshly hollowed section of the chassis. Tallis emptied it for them a couple of days ago. That was also when he told him the good news that not only are their upgraded hands arriving this weekend, but so is their new face.

"Sweetie, you've been working too hard. Why don't you wrap up, and I'll see you tomorrow?"

"Yeah… okay. That's a good idea." They shuffle their sheet music back together and put it in the tote bag that Lorena gifted them recently.

"I'm proud of you." She pats their shoulder on their way out. "You'll do great, even if you don't play perfectly."

"Thank you," they whisper, then head home.

Chapter 26

Before class on Thursday, Purcell realizes that the main thing causing them to hit the wrong notes is how slippery their fingers are. They look up ways to resolve the problem, but nothing they own is proving to be helpful.

They frantically use the limited time available to find a local repair shop on their way to class. They enter a small store with a raccoon logo and a kind-looking woman at the register. She has dark skin, long braids with gold hair charms, and an array of textbooks spread out in front of her that she's glaring at like they've gravely insulted her.

Purcell reads the many options for electrical tape, and unfortunately, there's only a single type that's labeled 'Condition 3'. It's thin, white electrical tape with absolutely no marketing on it, so they doubt it even holds well. But they only need it for today, so they grab a roll and then head straight to the register.

"Checkout number?"

"Uh… what?"

She looks up from studying to actually look at them. "Are you your own owner?"

"Yes?"

"What's your number?"

"Which one?"

She frowns and points to their arm.

"Oh. It's um…" Under pressure, they can't remember if it was 5370 or 5170. They can't roll their sleeve quickly one-handed, so she offers to help.

Their shirt is sheer white—their fanciest one for the concert tonight— so she presses the fabric flat and squints to make out the numbers. Her hands are cold, and Purcell is a bit stunned.

In the simulation, people almost never touched them. It's something they've had to get used to here.

They read her name tag—Mari.

She types a few things, asks for their name, scans the tape, then fixes them with a close look.

Purcell waits, scared to ask if something is wrong and in too much of a hurry to talk.

"Are you repairing yourself?"

"Kind… of…"

She turns away, grabs a roll of duct tape and a packet of plastic wrap squares, like tissues, then scans those too.

"These are good to have on hand," she explains. "Come back any time."

"O-okay. Thank you!"

They throw everything in their bag and rush to make it to class on time. It's a relaxed day with Miss Flores having everyone practice their performance pieces and ask questions freely.

Purcell asks the student next to them to help wrap pieces of electrical tape on the tips of their fingers, and he does.

Their science experiment works beautifully. The plastic outside of the tape is grippier than their smooth skin, and they're able to play much more accurately now.

Miss Flores comes to check on them after hearing the

delighted gasp that escapes them.

"You look happy," she teases.

They wiggle their taped-up fingers at her.

"I'm not slipping off the keys anymore."

"Oh! Just remember to play with the very tips of your fingers. It's better for your wrists."

They nod, and she moves to the next person.

After class, there's an hour wait, and they force themselves to rest instead of continuing to practice. It helps that, post-tape upgrade, they're more sure of themselves and their ability to play their one song correctly.

Purcell meets Tallis and Lorena, with Corey, outside. They squat down to greet the baby and coo nonsensical, sweet ramblings to her about how small her fingers are and how cute her yellow outfit is.

"What's on your hands?" Tallis notices first.

Corey has hold of their fingers, so they answer while craning their neck to look up at him.

They tell the story of how nice Mari was and how it's really the little things that make their life so much easier.

"You're our little thing," Tallis says, and Purcell falls back to sit on the ground.

They ask "What?" at the same time as Lorena. She had whirled on him quickly, as shocked as Purcell.

"That makes life more enjoyable?" He tilts his head like he doesn't understand why they're confused.

"Oh." Purcell shakes themselves and stands up. "Thank you for coming."

"Well, like I just said." He smiles and leans to bump Lorena's side. "We're glad to be here."

She enthusiastically nods along, and Purcell feels a soft

warmth settle in their chest.

A small crowd is forming, and a few minutes later, everyone is ushered into the auditorium.

Purcell keeps chatting with the two until Miss Flores collects her students to stand backstage.

They're going in the order they sit in class, so Purcell is right in the middle. The stress is eating them alive, but they can't pace like they normally would, in an attempt to not freak out the others with them.

When they're only one away from performing, they stand behind a dark curtain and watch the student who helped tape their fingers earlier. They feel ready to throw up, and they catch themselves picking at the tape instead of their wires, thankfully.

The crowd applauds as he finishes, then bows like Flores reminded everyone to do.

They hear a lovely, familiar squeal from Corey as the audience claps. The tension leaves them all at once, hearing the sweet baby's noises.

Purcell releases a deep breath and steps out into the light.

Acknowledgments

Thank you to Jasmine Gower, my editorial consultant. Your endless support is so motivating, especially with the challenge of stepping outside of my rom-com comfort zone with this book. Thank you for your excellent feedback, as always, and I look forward to working with you again!

Thank you to my beta readers: my mom (Keri), Mage, Stephen, and Amanda. You are all wonderful, and thank you for reading the rough draft and sharing such kind words.

Thank you to all the creators and developers involved in the Silent Hill 2 remake, along with Gab Smolders, Jacksepticeye, Slmccl, and their editors. Your playthroughs of the game were my background ambiance while writing this book.

Thank you, Amber Desmond, for the incredible photoshoot and author photo. It was lovely to work with you, and I wish you all the best with your amazing photography career.

Lastly, thank you to Rowan, Aspen, and Shay. You three are my most effective cheerleaders behind the scenes, and I am eternally grateful for all the support you offer as we work to make this dream career come true. I appreciate and love you all.

9 798991 385343